Suitcases

The Red-Letter Day

By SP McArdle

Illustrated by Kerry Hugill

SP PublishINK

SUITCASES: THE RED-LETTER DAY

© SP McArdle 2016

First published in 2016 by
SP.PublishINK
www.sppublishink.com

Text © SP McArdle 2016

Illustrations © Kerry Hugill 2016

The author has asserted her moral rights.

ISBN: 978-0-9935820-0-4

Cover illustration by Kerry Hugill.

Book and cover designed by SP McArdle, with assistance from Audrey Kane.

Printed in Poland by Drukarnia Skleniarz.

Contents

Acknowledgements

Thanks to Yasmin 'Aunty Jasmine' O'Grady for the writing course that sparked this novel trail in 2011 (my *Suitcases* books are set in the O'Grady farmhouse, complete with half-crocodile).

To Colleen Mirfin for listening so patiently.

To Claire Carry, Ros Drinkwater, Mary Anne Evans, Susan Lanigan, Heidi Murphy and Paul O'Rourke for their invaluable feedback.

To Maria Clowry, Moira Hannon, Louise Hughes, Naomi Richardson, Liz Rehmann and Karen Tracey for facilitating the focus group.

To Flick Henderson for the logo.

To Anne Hattaway, Audrey Kane and Paddy Lawlor for the final push.

To everyone who quietly believed I could do it, especially Mary Conroy and Pauline Fitzpatrick.

To so many wonderful writers and journalists for their kind words, including Anna Coogan, Eoghan Corry, Sinéad Crowley, Denise Deegan, Martina Devlin, Michelle Jackson, Madeleine Keane, Cathy Kelly, Sinéad Moriarty and Terry Prone (and to everyone I've left out – sorry).

To generous editors for the chance of publicity, especially Moira Hannon of the Irish Daily Star, Roslyn Dee and Linda Maher, the Irish Daily Mail and Claire McGovern, the Leitrim Observer.

And finally, eternal gratitude to the two Carolines – looking out for me always.

This Beginning

Jenny swiped her computer shut with an extra-clicky tut and an annoyed sigh. It was *no good.* The exact-right words for her supposedly exciting Easter essay wouldn't swim to the surface of her brain so her diving fingers could make them real.

And all those country corners and curves on the long drive to Aunty Jasmine and Uncle Donal's farmhouse meant she kept tapping the wrong letters anyway, regardless.

Mum turned and smiled a kindly 'I-told-you-not-to-use-your-computer-pad-in-the-car-so' smile just as Dad's eyes met Jenny's in the mirror with his consoling 'never mind' look which always cheered her up.

'I think the party will have started by now, Jenny,' said Mum briskly, as the car crunched up the farmhouse's gravel drive. 'Have you got Cousin Marilyn's birthday card and present ready?'

'Yes, Mum.' Jenny fished the crinkly parcel and crookedly-stuck-on pink envelope from her rucksack.

Cousin Tom was bang in the middle of a scrappy football match with his mates on the front lawn – and scowling nose-to-nose with an opposing attacker.

Hastily (and cleverly, Jenny thought) they both transformed their jabby pointing fingers into enthusiastic waves as Dad drove past.

'See you all after the game!' roared Tom, as Mum, Dad and Jenny got out of the car.

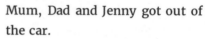

Jenny took a steadying deep breath and wondered how soon she could escape to the Best Bedroom of All.

The magic was calling her. The fingers on her left hand began to tingle, as if already turning the Best Bedroom's smooth hot doorknob.

It was almost time for another adventure!

Aunty Jasmine swung open the heavy front door at the precise moment Jenny's tingly fingers pressed the old-fashioned white porcelain bell (helpfully marked 'BELL' on the middle bell bit).

'Come in, come in, come *in*,' she beamed, her teeth pearly-white against her smooth brown skin.

She hugged Jenny tightly and swung her niece off the ground. 'The party's in the dining room.'

2

Jenny gave snarly Old Mrs Croc's dead half-body her customary kick in the hallway (the entire live crocodile had gotten on the wrong end of the deadly spear of a safari-loving far-distant relation of Aunty Jasmine at some point and, despite Jenny's probing questions every time she visited the farmhouse, nobody could tell her where, exactly or otherwise, the other half had ended up).

The noisy birthday party was in full swing and Jenny's eyes were drawn straight away to the huge table.

It was covered with so many cool fizzy drinks and platters of pointy sandwiches and plates of colourful iced cakes that you could only see odd spots of the pink polka-dot tablecloth.

'Jenny!' boomed Uncle Donal, striding over and pinging straight down on his lanky cartoon-like legs to hug his niece. 'Welcome, dear girl.'

Cousin Marilyn waved high from the centre of her chattering circle of friends.

'Hi, Jenny,' she trilled, emerging.

Jenny liked her tiny golden-haired cousin, but only in small doses. She *was* a lot younger, after all...

'Hello, Marilyn. Happy Birthday.'

Rrrrr-rrrr-iiiii-PPPPP

'Oh, *thanks*, Jenny – I *love* it!'

Cousin Marilyn had made short and untidy work

of unwrapping her present. 'Look, *look*, everyone!'

Jenny ducked as Cousin Marilyn began waving her brand-new sparkly wand and trying to step into the matching glittery fairy-princess tutu skirt at the very same time.

She'll fall over, thought Jenny (but with a kindly inside smile). *Marilyn always gets so excited!*

'Do have some sandwiches, Jenny,' invited Aunty Jasmine. 'Look, we've made lots of your favourite: cheese and pickle. Here you are.'

Squashing her impatience, Jenny sank into a worn velvet armchair at the fireplace to eat her party tea as the younger girls giggled around her in a gaggle.

Mum and Dad were chat-chat-chatting to Uncle Donal and some other parents while Aunty Jasmine hovered near the table, plucking a bun for someone's plate here and offering a napkin for someone's knee there.

I wonder... thought Jenny, finishing the last bite of her tasty sandwiches so fast that her fluttery adventure insides began to protest. *I wonder...*

The younger girls had all gone over to 'oooh' and 'aaaah' over Marilyn's pinker-than-pink cake before Aunty Jasmine took it away to light the candles.

I wonder if I could...

Dad, she signalled with her eyes.

4

But her father wasn't looking.

Mum! This time it worked.

'Hello, Jenny dear. Did you get enough to eat? Would you like something sweet now?'

'I'll get something later, Mum, thanks. After I go... You see, I'd really like to–'

'You can't leave Cousin Marilyn's party *already*, Jenny.' Mum shook her head firmly as she spoke. 'You've only just arrived.'

But Jenny wasn't giving up *that* easily. Both hands were tingling now. '*Please*, Mum. *Pleeeeease* let me go to the spare bedroom. Aunty Jasmine doesn't mind, and Marilyn certainly won't. *Look.*'

Mum smiled as she followed Jenny's pointed gaze to Cousin Marilyn, once more swallowed up by all her giggly girly friends.

'Yes, all right, Jenny. You may be excused once the birthday girl blows out her candles. But do it discreetly. Don't let anyone notice.'

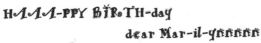

Cousin Marilyn's rosy cheeks huffed and puffed, but still the last candle spluttered for absolutely ages (or so it seemed to Jenny) before it went out.

*WH*oo–oo–oo*SH!*

Aunty Jasmine stepped forward, knife poised to cut into the frosty icing.

Jenny was free. At. Last.

Her heart flippedy-flipped as she picked up her rucksack and sidled quietly out of the dining room.

She skippety-skipped past the hallway fireplace with its stretched-out pointy antlers above (they always made her think of the twisted hands of a crabbed old giant waiting for his cup of tea).

And then past the snoozing black cat on the rug and onto the wooden staircase... upwards and onwards and towards Where It Happens.

Yooou've gooot the green light from Mum, so gooo fooor it, Jenny! Sensible Self was usually super-careful with her sound guidance – but not this bright Easter afternoon.

In fact, she followed up her hooty advice with a weird whoopity-cheer that Jenny had never heard before.

Hurry up, Jenny! Risky Self was usually super-carefree with *her* impatient orders – and today was no exception. She wheeled around on her roller skates in Jenny's head, trumpeting with enthusiasm.

The two selves in Jenny's mind who appeared in tricky situations – often trying to steer her in opposite directions, it must be said – were in rare agreement.

Jenny peeked into the other rooms off the landing because that's what she always made herself do before reaching the Best Bedroom – although this time she did it so quickly she barely saw inside.

1. Cousin Marilyn's pink palace ✓
2. Cousin Tom's soccer shrine ✓
3. Aunty Jasmine and Uncle Donal's comfy corner ✓

The doorknob of the Best Bedroom of All began to judder before Jenny could touch it. The door creakily opened by itself. It was *time*.

This adventure was about to begin!

The Beginning After That One

Jenny gazed up at the ancient brown suitcases with their tattered labels piled on top of the knotty old wardrobe to spot the...

Her heart sank.

Oh no! she thought. *Where's the little black hatbox? Why isn't it there?*

Jenny bit her lip, hard. No hatbox meant... meant *no adventure*.

The wardrobe (from where the crazy taps were emanating) began to shudder.

Its door creaked open – just a notch, and just for a moment. A paper aeroplane flew out, skidding past Jenny's worried face before sliding to a stop on the splodgy carpet beside her.

It's starting to happen, thought Jenny, grinning from ear to ear. *Brilliant!*

For a split second she felt torn between flinging open the wardrobe door and looking to see if there was a message on the paper plane telling her to do something else... but then... the paper began to flap itself flat... whereupon Jenny could clearly see the words *'OPEN ME'* scrawled in thick black marker pen.

That's strange, she thought, *the paper's already open. Hmmm.*

Tap, tappEty–tap, tap, TAP, TAP–*TAP–TAP!*

The wardrobe door scraped open again. Another paper plane shot low along the patterned carpet and halted beside Jenny's left foot.

Flap... flap... FLAP!

This paper, too, quickly flattened so she could see a message (typed, this time, and with such force that the 'O's had become holes).

The words were hardly flattering.

`'THE D●●R, Y●U SILLY GIRL'`

Oh, thought Jenny. *Oh, right.*

It wasn't a great beginning, as beginnings for her magical adventures went, but at least it was a start. And she really, really didn't want to have to sidle back into Cousin Marilyn's chatterbox-y birthday party again.

The **tap, tappEty–tap, tap, TAP, TAP–*TAP–TAPS*** struck up again as Jenny tugged open the heavy wooden wardrobe... to stare up, and up some more.

Her heart lifted as she saw what – or, more precisely, *who* – was in there.

Way, way high up inside, the cranky gnome was perched upon his round black hatbox home, which in turn was perched precariously on top of an uneven column of battered brown suitcases.

He was pounding at a dinky grey metal typewriter balanced upon his spindly knees.

Every wild swipe of his greeny-grey hands on the keys made the tower of assorted suitcases wobble and jiggle.

Jenny couldn't help laughing at this extraordinary sight, although – swiftly bringing to mind the fact that she needed the guidance of the Gnome in the Hatbox to go on her incredible journeys – covered her mouth and pretended to clear her throat instead.

'*Harummmph!*' Jeremiah Gnome flapped his warty tennis-racquet-sized feet as he glowered at Jenny. 'Yes, *yes* – what kept you so long *this* time?'

'Sorry, Jeremiah,' replied Jenny fake-humbly, but also so excited at the prospect of her next wonderful adventure that she couldn't help hopping from foot to foot. 'I had to go to Cousin Marilyn's birthday party first.'

The gnome's bulgy eyes gleamed as he rubbed his belly and began to drool and dribble down his several chins. (Ugh.) 'Did you bring me any cake?'

'Well-*llll* – erm – no, actually, you see... Aunty Jasmine hadn't quite begun to cu–'

Jeremiah sliced through Jenny's faltering explanation with a squelch of his rubbery lips, silently resuming his typing.

Jenny's heart sank. She stopped hopping, and almost – but not quite – stamped her foot.

If Jeremiah wouldn't tell her, how else was she to know which one was the adventure suitcase to step into and let the magical journey begin?

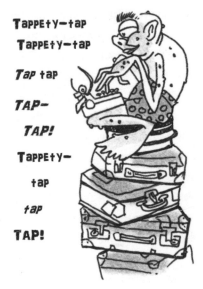

Tappety–tap
Tappety–tap

Tap tap

TAP–

TAP!

Tappety–

tap

tap

TAP!

Or what souvenirs she had to collect this time?

Or how she was to get home again?

As he flipped a skinny arm up and back to swipe at his sweaty head, Jeremiah's unsteady tower began to teeter and...

and... then... with the next tap, the very top toppled (thankfully this happened in slow motion, as things sometimes – and helpfully – did in her

11

adventures, to give Jenny a chance to save the day).

She seized the moment, catching the miniature typewriter in mid-air first and placing it gently on the carpet before doing the same for the bad-tempered gnome.

Despite his substantial pot belly, Jeremiah was surprisingly light and floppy.

His hatbox home bounced harmlessly across the floor before righting itself with a burpy slurp.

It raised its lid upright like an opened oyster.

The suitcases below the hatbox had stayed put, the falling-down part over (for now).

'*Harummmph!*' spluttered the Gnome in the Hatbox, sitting cross-legged in front of his rescued typewriter, his hands poised for more literary action.

'Can you help me please, Jeremiah?' asked Jenny firmly. '*Pleeease?*'

After all, she *had* more or less saved him from what might have been a very nasty injury. The least he could do was answer her key adventure questions.

'Which suitcase is my magic one this time? What souvenirs must I find? How do I get home, please?'

The gnome sniggered, but not unkindly so.

He nodded quite specifically back over his shoulder towards a battered suitcase at the very bottom of the pile, took a deep, exaggerated breath like an actor would in a hammy play, and puffed himself up to practically double his original size.

'Ahhh-hhhhh-hemmm,' he gargled.

Jenny swallowed a giggle. *Jeremiah looks even more ridiculous than usual*, she thought.

'Ahhh-ha-AAA-*HEMMMMM!*'

Tugging a piece of paper from his typewriter, the Gnome in the Hatbox proclaimed as follows:

WHENNN/ YOU FINNND/
THE SPECIAL PARCHMENNN-T/
AND PENNNNNNNN *(AH-HA-HEMMM)*
MAKE THEM WORK IN UNIONNN/
ANNND TOUCH THE/
FINISHED FREEDOM DOCUMENNN-T/
YOU CANNN/ COME HOME/
AGAINNNNNNN

Hmmm. Jenny frowned. *That's not much to go on and it's not very clear either,* she thought. *Do I bring the special paper and pen back to Jeremiah Gnome as souvenirs, then?*

She decided it's always better to ask, especially as Mum often said that making assumptions was the road to nowhere.

'Do I have to bring the–?'

'Yes, yes, you do,' snapped the gnome, flexing and cracking his lanky fingers before filling his typewriter with paper once more and drumming ferociously at the keys.

'How will I get to EACH new PART of the ADVENTURE?' Jenny had to shout above the rising din.

Jeremiah snorted but then – as Jenny realised was his habit, for she had witnessed this many times before – relented.

He ripped a sheet of paper from his typewriter, crumpled it up into a sloppy ball and hurled it towards his hatbox home.

Whereupon an ancient book rose from the depths of the hatbox, gently and dignifiedly opened its musty pages with a knowing sigh and... and swallowed the papery blob into what Jenny could only properly describe as a black hole!

Jeremiah Gnome winked and nodded at Jenny as he threw screwed-up ball after screwed-up ball of paper into the apparently bottomless depths of the ancient book.

And then... and then he sprang up and dived right into it after them all!

Jenny's jaw dropped. She was dumbfounded.

Is he coming back? Surely he must come back! Panic and disappointment rose into her throat.

I wanted to ask him about my guide for this adventure. And what the 'freedom document' is...

Oh, and Jeremiah didn't press my watch to make it magic – so am I not going back in time this time? This is NO GOOD at ALL. I need to KNOW!

Jenny took a deep slow counting breath, knowing this always helped.

It was time for Sensible Self to row in with her opinion, which she sensibly (and hootily) did.

You knooow enough, Jenny. If the gnome is nooot coming back you can still have yooour adventure. You don't need to knooow everything. You learned that in the clooock tower adventure, remember?

Jenny took another deep breath. Her alarm bells began to fade.

It *was* only the beginning, after all, and – as she well knew – those were often tricky.

If Sensible Self thought everything was all right, then it must truly be.

The wardrobe's leaning tower of suitcases began to shudder and rumble.

The one the cranky gnome had given his adventure nod to shot out smoothly from the very bottom, almost as far as the door of the Best Bedroom of All.

The suitcase's lid flipped up with a welcoming creak and began to flap.

Step in, Jenny, urged Risky Self, her roller skates

whirring with anticipation in Jenny's rapidly steadying head. *Get on with it!*

So – even though she didn't know as much as she'd like to in this particular Beginning – Jenny did exactly, and adventurously, that.

Almost
Chapter One

'AAAARRRRGHHHHHH!' Swirling winds whistled around Jenny's ringing ears as, eyes squeezed shut, ankles tightly crossed and every muscle in her body clenched, she clung on for dear life to wherever this was.

She could feel cold metal beneath her stretch-clasped icy hands as her long hair whipped and snaked madly around her head (like witches' stringy locks might in the windiest fairy tale you ever read, for example).

And really, if truth be told, right now Jenny was wishing she wasn't a brave adventuress-stroke-explorer at all any more.

But all brave adventuresses etc always need to get their bearings, so she opened her eyes.

And then (oh, *dear*)... looked down.

'Ooooo-OOOOOO*HHHH!*' squealed Jenny, her head spinning.

She was perched at the very, very, *very* top of

'What was in the room at the end of the awesome library?'

some kind of super-tall spire in the middle of a busy city street.

'Send me BACK!' wailed Jenny, closing her eyes again. 'Send me *BACK*! Jer-E-MI-AAAA*HHHH*!'

The blustering gale grabbed her plea and taunted her with fleeting echoes.

... 'AAA*HHH* ...
... '*AAHH*' ...

'AH – I say, this simply won't do at all.'

Jenny's eyes flew open again as she realised the echo hadn't been her, after all.

'Oh!' she exclaimed.

And then, when she saw who indeed it had been, a much louder and surprised '*OH!*'

'You're *blue*,' she whispered to a shimmery-shaped man in a suit hovering brightly against the dull city sky.

He was probably about the same age as Jenny's father and her uncle Donal, but with floppy hair and plump shapely lips any film star would be proud of (especially the older ones).

Goodness, thought Jenny. *He seems familiar. I wonder if he's famous. Is he my guide for this adventure, then? Hmmm. I hope he knows how to get me down off this spike thingy.*

Floppy Hair looked solemn, although his eyes smiled. 'Dear, *dear* girl, this just won't *do*. You're in the wrong *place* at the wrong *time*.'

With that, and before Jenny could ask any questions about blue-ness or anything else, he reached out and pressed her wristwatch.

Whiz, whizz, WHIZZZ, *WHIZZZZZ*!

The four date slots on her watch immediately began to whiz back from that day's date...

'AH, this is *much* more like it. Home rules and all that. Inside the good old campanile – that's a bell tower to you, my dear. A belfry, if you prefer. Follow me, if you please. It's not far.'

Floppy Hair – for it was he, although seriously younger and not a bit blue any more – strode purposefully out of the arched bell tower and onto a smooth lawn.

He was wearing a flowing black graduation-type gown, identical to the flowing gowns worn by the very many other men and boys scurrying about and across the grassy square.

Jenny hastily followed suit, while – as she always did anywhere new – looking around, and in this case slightly back as well, to get her bearings.

They had landed within the most beautifully

intricate bell tower Jenny had ever seen (not that she had seen many), but built on the ground instead of on top of a church or temple.

The campanile went up and across and in again like a tiered cake, with statues and rounded steps and curvy window shapes on every layer.

The bobbly bit on the very top – which also had even tinier curved windows – even reminded Jenny of a giant cherry on top.

The belfry was on a square lawn surrounded on all sides by stately ivy-covered buildings with columns and turrets and arches and all other kinds of terribly important architectural stuff.

This is definitely an ancient university, thought Jenny. *I'm sure I've seen it before... perhaps on the television news? Hmmm.... or maybe in a film?*

She stifled a laugh. *They look like giant bats, racing around like that in their gowns. Why, they're bats in the belfry!*

Still grinning at her own joke, Jenny stared down at her watch. One-eight-seven-one.

So it's 1871. Well, the university part certainly makes sense now, given that my souvenirs for this adventure are a special parchment and pen.

As Floppy Hair had slowed to a stroll and Jenny was only a half-step behind him, she decided to try to find out a bit more. 'Excuse me–?'

Just then an out-of-breath student, possibly the

handsomest person Jenny had ever seen, dashed up, waving a large ink-spattered roll of bright yellow paper.

'I say...' *(paNt, WHeeze)* '...old chap, any chance you can...' (*WHeeze, paNt*) '...help me with this blasted ess–'

Floppy Hair interrupted with an irritated tut. 'No time, Dorian,' he snapped, pausing. 'You'll have to write it yourself this time, old man. I certainly won't. Must fly.'

He turned on his heel to sidestep Handsome Dorian, a stiff breeze filling his gown, and muttered, 'Ugly piece of work. *Pah!*'

At this, the two forked bits of Handsome Dorian's stiff white shirt collar poking out from above his college robe appeared to hiss like snakes' tongues.

Jenny shrank back behind Floppy Hair, as most people would – even brave adventuresses like her.

Handsome Dorian's eyes narrowed as he stepped sideways to look her up and down with disdain.

'*Whaaat* do we have hee-*eere*?' His voice rose and fell in a most sinister manner.

'*Women* – never mind *girls* – aren't allowed here yet, dear chap,' sneered Dorian. 'You know the rules. Now, I might be tempted to rat on you, unless...'

He slapped the yellow parchment scroll against one shoulder with a malicious wink.

Goodness, he's a real baddie, thought Jenny, realising Dorian's sly intention. *He* looks *handsome, but it's a different story underneath. That's blackmail!*

Floppy Hair folded his arms and frowned.

'He's right,' he murmured, more to himself than anyone else. 'I'll need to disguise her so we can...'

Pointing to Not-So-Handsome-Underneath Dorian's university gown, he snapped: 'If you please, old chap. I'll write the essay for you in exchange.'

In a trice Jenny was swathed in the gown, her long hair tucked in under the top – and fervently hoping none of the scurriers-past had noticed her.

It's a good job horrible Dorian is small for his age and I'm tall for mine, she thought. *His cape thingy almost covers my red trainers – great!*

Stuffing the unfinished essay inside his jacket, Floppy Hair set off at a trot towards the biggest and most ornately columned of the stately buildings.

'Ooooohhhhh,' whispered Jenny, once they had rushed through the stained-glass round foyer part at the front of it (this is called a rotunda, if anyone ever asks you). '*Ooooohhhhhhh!*'

For this was a place of pure enchantment.

There were soaring shelves upon soaring shelves displaying one of her most favourite things (which included chocolate cheesecake and cheesy action films, so you get the picture of how good *this* was).

Yes, floors and floors and *floors* of bookshelves, as far up as her keenly craning neck could look at.

Up and over and down and up – Jenny's eyes roved around as if trying to solve a giant crossword.

Thick and thin and brown and black and... *ooooh*... (If she hadn't been on an adventure, Jenny could have kept gazing around this wondrous library for much, much, *much* longer than she actually did.)

Floppy Hair was staring longingly at everything as well.

Then, shaking his head and shrugging his shoulders with a sigh, he steered Jenny towards a room at the end of the cavernous library.

Thankfully everyone else present had had their noses buried in a book, as bookworms tend to do, and didn't take a blind bit of notice of the robed pair.

There was only one thing in the dim vaulted room they entered – a tall display cabinet – and only one thing in that – an opened book with complicated capital letters and beautiful drawings punctuated by flowing writing in a dense foreign language.

Creee-aaa-aa-KKKKKK!

Floppy Hair opened the heavy glass door and carefully placed the book on the floor. Kneeling, he swept his hands into a downward loop for Jenny to step onto. 'Off you go, dear girl. Dive in.'

But Jenny kept both feet firmly on the ground.

Much as she loved books – and although this was clearly what Jeremiah Gnome had been showing her earlier on – it seemed a very risky move indeed.

What if the book doesn't let me dive in and I bang my head instead? she thought. *I know nothing about Floppy Hair, after all. He could be a baddie, too!*

He's not. He's yoooour friend. Ask him.

Thanks, Sensible Self, thought Jenny. *I'll do that.*

Floppy Hair, still waiting to propel Jenny head-first into the ancient book, appeared lost in thought as he gazed at its ornately penned pages.

'Hang on a moment, please,' said Jenny firmly. 'I have a few questions, if you don't mind.'

'Not at all, dear girl,' he replied kindly. 'I quite understand. I always like to know everything about my new friends, and nothing about my old ones.'

Jenny couldn't help grinning at the funny cleverness of this remark. 'Am I your friend, then?'

'Indeed thus, m'dear. I am your guide for this entire adventure.'

'So are you going to dive into the book after me?'

'Why, of course. I can resist everything except temptation.'

'What's your name?

'You may call me... O... O'Flahertie.'

Oh, Floppy O'Flahertie – that's hilarious!

What are you waiting for? Risky Self screeched up in Jenny's head on her roller skates and began clattering the clunky heel-wheels against each other with teeth-grinding impatience.

He's really clued-in, and he's coming with you to sort everything out as you go along. Don't be such a scaredy-cat – get on with it!

Jenny drew a deep, deep breath, quelled her heady question marks (for now at least), folded the robe into her rucksack in case it caught on anything... and put herself into O'Flahertie's hands.

POU-FFFFFFF! WHᵒᵒᵒ-*OOOOSH!*

Chapter One

Jenny blinked. And blinked once more again, to be sure. To be sure. *Hmmm*, she wondered. *I can't see a thing. Where on earth am I? Where's O'Flahertie?*

She stretched a faltering hand into the silent darkness before her and–

'*Oh!*' Jenny's fingertips had encountered something roughly familiar.

It felt like... yes, it felt exactly like the bark of a tree. But as Jenny's hand crept along, to the right, the left, and then back to the right again, she realised the curve was *the wrong way round!*

'I *can't* be...' Jenny wasn't panicking just yet (although it was fair to say that she might be, soon).

'Could I... could I possibly be *inside*?' she whispered faintly to herself.

'The truth is rarely pure and never simple.'

'*Oh* – O'Flahertie!'

Jenny turned towards her guide's voice in the rounded darkness as fast circles of dull light began to appear through the tree's knotholes.

'You're *green*!' she exclaimed, her eyes

'The party in the forest clearing had started with a bang'

welcoming (a) the glow of a rising moon and (b) O'Flahertie's colourful glimmery outline.

He was sitting on a knotty shelf inside the tree (for yes, that is precisely where the adventurous pair had landed into just now, whenever 'now' was).

Legs crossed and with one elegant hand gently drumming on the sticking-out tip of his topmost knee, Jenny's guide seemed oddly relaxed in such strange circumstances.

He looked the same age as his student self in 1871, but...

'Why are you *green?*'

O'Flahertie pointed to Jenny's wristwatch, which had vibrated madly as she dived into the book.

Between (a) and (b) she could just about decipher the numbers on the four date slots, but...

The slot on the left-hand side was blank!

'Eight-oh-six. Eight-oooooh-*sixxxxx?*' Jenny's voice rose in a great deal of surprise. She had fully expected another number in *that* equation.

Really and truly, her adventures had never occurred so very long ago before.

And she really wasn't sure about this one – *at –* ALL, this time!

Jenny's stomach began to flutter as her mind flew in several directions at once.

'Could we be... could we be back in *prehistoric* times?' she squeaked.

Her watch buzzed again. The letters 'A' and 'D' filled the empty date slot.

Whew, that's a relief!

Jenny wasn't entirely sure how well she would cope with an adventure that might involve dinosaurs and cave people running around grunting instead of speaking.

'Do stop panicking, dear girl.' O'Flahertie's tone was brisk. 'Here, peep through this knothole. It's about to be exceedingly hilarious. Actually, it's *already* hilarious – but you cannot hear it until you look.

'You are most fortunate to be an adventuress, believe me,' he added gravely. 'To *live* is the rarest thing in the world. Most people *exist*, that is all.'

'But why are you...?'

'Why am I this colour? Why, because I haven't been born yet. And I was blue in the sky because that was during your time but after mine, don't you know.'

Hmmm, thought Jenny, settling down rapidly at O'Flahertie's no-nonsense attitude. *Well, that makes some sense, I suppose. But shouldn't I be...?*

'Shouldn't I be green as well then, if that's how it works?' she asked. 'I haven't been born yet, either.'

'Oh, certainly,' replied O'Flahertie. 'No idea why that didn't happen. Although if I may say so,

30

m'dear, I really don't think that particular hue would suit you. In my view you should remain the exception to the rule: in the pink, as it were.'

Then, looking shifty on top of his usual clever seriousness, he folded his arms and began drumming long fingers on his smooth chin.

'Now, let me see if I can recall how it is done. It most definitely involves magic...

'Oh, let me *think*... Hocus-focus... No, that isn't right *at all*. Abra-*kebab*-bra...'

Jenny turned towards the nearest hole in the grainy tree bark. 'It's fine,' she snapped. 'Forget it.'

I don't think O'Flahertie can do proper magic at all, she thought with an irritated sniff. *Some guide he is. Well, he had better not let me down if things get tricky later on.*

Biting her lip, Jenny pressed her face against the tree and looked all around in the moonlight to get her bearings as best she could.

The forest was creaking and whistling in a truly magical, *alive* way.

Emerald-green bobbly moss and shiny mushrooms grew almost everywhere and raindrops dripped off glistening branches and plants.

As Jenny's eyes widened in awe, flowers in rainbow colours opened and closed, swayed and danced.

Then:

BANGGG! BAAANNN *GGGGG!*

And then:

HiSSSSS. SizZZZZZLe.

HiSSSSSS-_SSSSSS_

Twwangggggggg. **D**uff, **D**uffEtY-*DUFF,* **D**uff.

Plus: **P**Linkety-*PL/NK! TWANNNNNG*-**D**uff.

PLink-*PL/NK*-twannnn- *GGGGGG!*

Mixed in with:

𝔅la--bla--bla--*𝔅L𝒜*--bla-bla-blaaa

Followed by:

BLaa---bLaa--BLAA--BL**A**AAAA-*BLAA*-bLaa-bLaaaa

Oh, and:

Bongggggg. **D**uff-**D**uff-***DUFF*!!**

WHeee-EEEeeeeee-EE!

𝔅ongggggg...

Thud-tHud-DEtY-**D**uff-tHud-**DD**-D-D...

And not forgetting:

***B**ong, **P**Link, **T**hud, H**i**ss, Twang, **D**uff, SizZLe, 𝔅ong*

There were so many noises crammed together
that Jenny's ears could hardly take them all in.

32

She skirted around O'Flahertie and peered out.

BannᴳᴳGG

BANG-ETY-*BANGGGGG!*

Ba-Bannᴳᴳᴳ-*GGGGGGG!*

The party in the forest clearing on the opposite side of their tree had, most definitely, started with a bang.

This was another world entirely. A huge blackened pig stuck on a spit sizzled over a bright crackling fire, spitting fat up and down and sideways.

A stout monk was slowly turning the spit with one hand, holding a massive plate in the other – and hopping and yelping every time spurts of hot fat hit his sandalled feet.

Four equally portly monks waited in a nearby semi-circle, their own small plates outstretched and their begging eyes as wide as saucers.

Jenny turned her eyes next to stare at a band of brown-robed brothers off to the left.

Some were dancing so wildly in the din that the tufts of hair all around the shaved crowns of their heads flapped up and down like tiny birds learning to fly.

The rest of the rest were enthusiastically creating the aforementioned din, which appeared music to their ears (but certainly no-one else's).

33

'I adore simple pleasures,' muttered O'Flahertie, clamping his hands over his own ears, 'but this confounded racket is, quite simply, *painful* in its complexity.'

To accompany the out-of-tune singing, one wannabe music-making monk was swinging around a woodworm-riddled harp, plucking the strings with his teeth whenever he passed close enough.

Two more in his merry band of brothers jiggled what looked like guitars against their bellies, with long stretches between each straggly strum as they fiercely debated what chord to attempt next.

DUFF–DUFF–*PLISH*–*PLISH*–DUFF–DUFF–
BanG–*BANGGETY*–*BANG*–PLISSS–SSHHH

On hearing this much more all-together sound, Jenny checked the numbers and letters on her watch. It was definitely still 806AD.

'Look, O'Flahertie,' she urged. '*Look!*'

Her guide slowly took his fingers out of his ears, opened his scrunched-up eyes and stood up.

The final monk they could see (for now) was bashing like crazy at a shiny drum kit, complete with clashing cymbals.

It was a totally modern set, as professional as a world-famous band would use!

O'Flahertie didn't seem at all fazed by this untimely contradiction, remarking: 'Dear girl, I can believe anything, provided that it is quite incredible.'

'You're incredibly clever yourself, O'Flahertie,' replied Jenny, so impressed with her guide's matter-of-fact take on events that she was prepared to overlook his terrible attempt at magic.

'Why don't you write a book with all your witty sayings in it?'

'M'dear, I am too fond of reading books to care to write them.'

Yet a yearning expression crossed his face like a lonely cloud as he said it. 'Perhaps...'

With that, O'Flahertie sat back down on his handy seat-ledge and began scratching frantically at the tree bark with a fluffy white feather.

Тнимр... *THUMPP...* **THUMPPP!**

Plants and flowers and trees shook with each giant footstep approaching from afar (for yes, that was the reason behind the thumping).

A hasty silence fell as the spit-turning monk hastily stopped spit-turning.

He pulled a jagged wooden dagger from behind the ropey belt of his brown habit and began carving chunks off the pig, piling them onto the plate he had been holding at the ready.

Immediately the four semi-circular monks rose and held out their smaller ones, slavering wildly.

'*Wait*, dear brethren,' scolded the stout head chef. 'Our gentle giant must eat his fill first.'

Tutting and huffing and puffing, the four retreated as the din-making brothers began to gather around the spitting campfire.

WOOF-**THUMP,** WOOF-*THUMPP!* (And so on.)

The two sounds grew louder and closer, until...

'Ohhhhhh!' Jenny jumped back towards the centre of the tree as a shiny black eye (not an unfriendly one, it must be said, just large and unexpected) almost blocked her peephole.

The air was filled with the sound of panting and slobbering.

'*HERE, BOY! SIT!*'

The booming command came from a bearded wild-haired warrior-type giant (well, almost as big as a house, so not *absolutely* huge).

This medium-sized giant was dressed in a mishmash of animal skins and woolly layers of tartan in many shades of one particular colour.

He was greeted with roars of approval from the monks, most especially the four hungry ones.

The slobbering was from a massive hound – easily larger than a horse – with a shaggy brown coat, long nose, lolling tongue and waggy tail.

The stout chef proudly proffered the heaped plate to the giant, who grunted in appreciation.

'That giant warrior-man looks really cool, but why is he *red all over*?' whispered Jenny, peering out again.

O'Flahertie stopped scratching. 'Why, my dear, because he's mythical. The stuff of legends, don't you know.'

'Fair enough.' Jenny was ready to believe anything after the drum-kit episode. 'But why is the dog not, then?'

Her guide pulled a face. 'He's *definitely* real, dear girl. You'll find out just *how* real in a moment. Ugh!'

Jenny didn't much like the sound of *that*.

'Who *is* everyone, O'Flahertie?'

'Oh *my*, dear girl, if I told you *that* it would be *far* too easy,' he replied. 'Fear not, you'll figure it out sometime. If not now, whenever...'

I'll try more questions later if I can, decided Jenny. *Maybe he'll let something slip then.*

Mythical Man settled awkwardly on a fallen tree trunk to wolf down his dinner, throwing occasional scraps to his faithful hound, who did ditto.

Suddenly he halted, a juicy morsel at his lips. 'WHERE IS-?' he called, looking puzzled and around. 'O, BROTHER, where *ART* thou?'

'He is working, as per his usual habit,' replied the stout spit-turner with a most impatient tsk-tsk. 'I shall fetch him anon. Tsk-tsk. Tsk-*tsk-TSK!*'

As the fire calmed, the four hungry monks edged steadily closer to the crackling pig, greedy eyes on the medium giant making short work of his dinner.

Just then a lean poker-faced brother nibbling on a carrot wandered into the clearing and clambered up on the tree trunk beside the giant.

'Greetings, oh mighty hunter-gatherer Finn McCool,' he intoned. 'Thine presence is most timely.' (CHOMP, NibbLe.) 'For verily I have no more treated parchment left...' (NibbLe, CHOMP) '...for the next volume of my sacred scripture.'

'CONNNSIDER it DONNNE, my learned FRIENNND,' thundered Finn McCool, finishing his hearty meal in one fell swoop. 'I will journey ACROSS for IT!'

(Whereupon the ravenous monks gave him filthy looks and fell upon their own delayed feast.)

'Will Horrible Dorian's essay parchment do?' asked Jenny. 'Should we squeeze it out of the tree?'

'Ah no, dear girl,' replied O'Flahertie, 'it's absolutely the wrong colour and from the wrong time. Never mind being covered in ugly ink blots, don't you know. But thank you nonetheless.'

'I shall set off IMMEDIATELY to fetch it from thy fellow learned brethrennn FAR AWAY,' boomed the mythical giant, leaping up.

'Oh no, O'Flahertie,' whispered Jenny. 'That sounds amazing and we're going to miss it stuck in this tree. How on earth are we going to get out?'

(Actually this had been bothering Jenny since they arrived in 806 AD in the first place, but, being a brave adventuress and all, she had tried not to worry about it.)

WHEEEEEEEEEEE–*EEEEEEE!*

The whistle was so piercing that Jenny's ears rang, rang and rang some more... oh, for ages after that.

'FUAL! *FINNND!*'

Pinching his nose, O'Flahertie edged gingerly towards the centre of the tree and wrapped his robe tightly around him with a shudder.

'What's happening?' asked Jenny, alarmed. 'Why is Mythical Man calling his dog a fool? Who *is* he, anyway? Is something up?'

'Od yes, dear gird. Someding's up all righd. Id's up as a number-one prioridy for de dog, who's no fool ad all, by de way.'

During O'Flahertie's muffled words the giant's enormous wolfhound had bounded back towards their tree bark, his glistening nose quivering.

Jenny scooted in beside her guide, heart pounding. *'Get us out of here!'* she whispered.

But then – oh, dear – then something *was* up (as in: the dog's leg was!).

A burning chemical-y stink invaded the tree, making Jenny's eyes water. She held her nose, but it was too late.

Then: **THUMP!**
        THUMP!
                THUMPPP!

Three strides had taken Finn McCool to within a wild whisker of Jenny and her guide.

'FUAL has *CHOSENNN!*' he boomed, patting his oddly named dog. 'I shall RETURNNN in good *TIME* with thy PARCHMENNNT *from the SPECIAL TREE!*'

'Hang on tightly, Jenny,' warned O'Flahertie, hooking his fingers into the handiest knotholes and bracing his body wide against the inside tree trunk.

Thankfully Jenny did the white-knuckled same on the opposite inside, for...

...with two sharp tugs, Finn McCool ripped their tree out of the ground and tucked it under his arm!

The journey that followed was so utterly and phantasmagorically wondrous that Jenny often wondered if she imagined some of it.

Through her roomy sideways peephole she spied moonbeams moving like spotlights over crisp fields bursting with luscious grapes, ripe corn and swaying daffodils as Finn raced on and Fual galloped behind.

When they halted, Jenny smelled salty sea air before she saw curly white tops of waves and heard surf sucking in and out.

Mythical Man did say it was far away, she thought. *We must be going to another country. Great!*

Splashhhh…..SPLISHHHH…..splaaashhh….. SPLISHHHH…..SPLAAASHHH….SPLISSSSH

With the chosen tree still snugly under his arm, the mythical warrior hurled boulder after boulder into the sea with one powerful arm, making a rocky path straight across.

Then he tossed in several more rocks either side of that (just for good luck, you might say).

Finn McCool and his faithful companion began pounding over this surprisingly steady homemade causeway as the two stowaways clung on tightly to either side of the inside tree.

Jenny caught glimpses of singing mermaids moonbathing on smooth seas, multi-coloured dolphins leaping for the stars, and whirring dinosaurs flapping veiny wings against the sky.

(You must make up your own minds whether Jenny did imagine some of this, but at the very least she insists the mermaids were definitely there.)

'Wheeeeee,' she yelled, above all the pounding and splashing and (possible) singing and whirring. *'Wheeee-EEEEEEE!'*

'Are you all RIGHT, dear *GIRL?*' screeched O'Flahertie.

'Yes, THANKS! Oh LOOK, we're on *LAND* again. This is *FANTAST– aaarg-HHH...*'

Finn McCool had stopped so dead that Fual bumped into him with a surprised yelp.

'I CANNNNNOT *BELIEVE–*'

With a horrified gasp the medium giant gently set the chosen tree on its side upon the ground.

He stooped his head and strode into a huge stone hut, sighing.

Fual ran off out of sight, howling.

'Hurry, Jenny,' urged O'Flahertie, clambering out of the bottom of the tree and nimbly avoiding its tangled roots. 'Follow me, if you please.'

But Jenny didn't move. She figured it would take a lot to upset Finn McCool – and he clearly *was* extremely upset.

So whatever had happened (or, even worse, was *still* happening) must be truly dire. She was staying put until she knew more.

Yooou can't stay in there, hooted Sensible Self. *Come ooout!*

I agree, snapped Risky Self. *Apart from the general scaredy-cat-ness of it, how will you find your parchment and pen souvenirs, make them work together and get home to Mum and Dad again?*

That was quite enough to make Jenny snap out

42

of it. She wriggled out onto the grass and steeled herself for whatever was to follow.

Brushing night-dew off her jeans and jumper, and with her heart pumping loudly in her head, Jenny looked around as O'Flahertie waited patiently nearby.

They were in a small village with stone huts shaped like beehives (or igloos, if you prefer a cooler version) on top of a low hill overlooking a lapping moonlit sea.

But...

Many of the huts were in ruins. Broken pottery lay everywhere among the spread-out ashes of a long-dead campfire.

O'Flahertie pointed to the ginormous beehive-stroke-igloo hut-building – still thankfully intact – Finn had entered and put a finger to his lips.

'Come along. But *shhhhh.*'

They could hear the mythical giant stomping about inside, shouting.

'Can you make us invisible?' pleaded Jenny. '*Pleeease?*'

'Dear me no, dear girl,' replied O'Flahertie, tiptoeing forward with a grimace. 'The true mystery of the world is in the visible, not the invisible.'

He's a totally useless *guide,* thought Jenny, quite reversing her earlier impressed opinion. *I bet he doesn't even* know *any invisibility spells!*

'All will be well, my dear. I promise. Now *shhhh*.'

Screeeeecchhhhh! The sound of roller skates in Jenny's head was unmistakable.

All right, all right, *Risky Self,* she replied firmly. *You can stop right there. I'm getting on with it.*

The pair waited until the giant's sounds were furthest away and then sidled in through the door.

It was an awesome printing workshop, with thingamabob machines and contraptions of all sizes far too complicated to describe properly.

Metal measures of all sizes and shapes hung around the walls, and rows and rows of shelves were crammed with jars and bottles of neatly labelled chemicals and types of ink.

It was the tidiest, most well-organised place Jenny had ever seen – and most especially compared to the dreadful chaos outside.

'Under here,' hissed O'Flahertie, pulling Jenny under a low bench as Mythical Man strode closer, furiously sweeping several dusty books off a shelf into a furry pouch slung across his body.

His wild locks brushed the ceiling and his red skin and clothes sizzled redder with rage and frustration.

'I do not *KNNNOW* how to *MAKE IT*,' he roared, crouching to glare at a jar labelled *BARIUM* in flowing script, then to stare at another marked 'SULPHUR'. 'I cannot *BELIEVE* the monks are *GONNNNE!*'

'What's he looking for?'

'The special formula to treat the parchment,' replied O'Flahertie in hushed tones. 'But the monks over here have fled and he doesn't know where it is.'

Given the workshop's gazillions of containers, from teeny-tiny to gargantuan, Jenny agreed that it was no wonder Finn McCool was in such a state. She felt very sorry for him indeed.

'Do *you* know?' she retorted, fully expecting a negative answer after the whole invisibility fiasco.

'Oh yes,' affirmed her guide airily. 'I shall show him directly.'

With that O'Flahertie shimmied out from under the bench and crossed the workshop by darting nimbly between several tallish machines.

He inched towards a bubbling bell jar on the ground and turned it around so that 'PARCHM' inscribed on the label was clearly visible in bold and beautiful CAPITALS. Then O'Flahertie pulled the cork stopper from the jar and ducked out of sight.

Urrrrghhhhh, thought Jenny, trying not to breathe too deeply. *What a stink!*

Finn McCool stopped in his tracks at the other end of the workshop and followed his nose back.

45

'A–HA!' he bellowed, racing outside to break his set-down tree into pieces and carry them in.

See-SaW-SEEEE-SAW-*SEEEEE-SAWWWWWW*

*Splurggggh-gghhh-*GHHHHH

Ker-PLONGGGG-GG-*GGGGGGG*

Goodness, thought Jenny. *Mythical Man certainly knows what he's doing now!*

With many energetic movements the giant fed the tree parts into contraption after thingamabob – pouring the °PARCHM° solution into the top of the last machine and pressing a red button.

GLUg-GLuGG–*gurrrr*-GGLE-GURGGGGLLE.

A roll of dull yellowy-red parchment fell out of the final machine into Finn McCool's waiting hands.

The legendary warrior nodded with satisfaction.

'The learned *brethrennn* who laboured in this place with such *reverennnce* would be proud, but I fear they are lost forever,' he said in a choked voice, putting down his hard-earned prize to wipe his eyes.

Blinking back her own tears, Jenny was sadly sure Mythical Man was dead right. *Surely this is my first souvenir,* she thought next. 'O'Flahertie, is th–?'

Her guide nodded. 'Cover your ears, Jenny.'

Finn McCool was pursing his lips again. It was even louder than before.

WHeeeEEEEeeeee–*EEEEEE*

'FUAL! *HERE!*'

'Follow me, if you please, dear girl.'

Once Jenny's ears had stopped ringing and screeching, and after an important moment spent doing something else as a result, she followed her guide outside

'Excellent,' whispered O'Flahertie, as Jenny fiddled with her rucksack clasps. 'I was about to ask you to put on your robe.'

'Oh – erm – certainly.' Jenny gave a guilty start as if that had been her exact intention all along.

The robed pair hid in the moon shadow of a ruined hut as the giant's faithful wolfhound bounded in to his master, woofing enthusiastically.

Then (oh, dear):

Pisssshhhhhhh-*hisss*-*SSSSSSS*

The pong of chemicals was worse (if that were humanly possible) than it had been inside the tree when the dog marked it out as his number-one parchment choice.

'Good *BOY!*' Finn McCool emerged from the printing works with the dripping parchment – now much more red than yellow – held aloft. 'You have COMPLETED the *PROCESS*, clever *FUAL!*'

He waved the treated paper in the night air to dry it, then rolled it up and tucked it safely (for now) between the books stowed in his animal-skin pouch.

He secured the pouch on Fual's furry back with a long strip of red tartan (which, believe it or not, turned into a blue-and-green version of itself the instant it touched the dog).

Finally, Finn McCool gave an anguished look around the monks' ruined village before striding towards the beach.

'On my say-so, *JUMP!*' ordered O'Flahertie, signalling his intention to Jenny. 'I shall go first.'

As Fual trotted past, Jenny's guide leaped up, his university gown filling with air. He landed as gracefully as a ballerina on the dog's back.

'*JUMP!*'

Jenny immediately followed suit, but – oh, dear – the least said about *her* clumsy landing, the better.

Either way, Fual was no fool. He was *not* impressed.

WOOOOO-*FFFFFFF!* GRRRR-*RRRRR!*

The wolfhound growled over one shoulder, the hackles on his shaggy back rising.

'What if he bucks us off and bites us?' hissed Jenny, settling in behind O'Flahertie as best she could in such ungainly circumstances.

'Ah no, dear girl – that's not in his call of nature at all.'

'Are you *sure*?

'Yes, indeed. However, to be sure, to be sure, I have a clear solution.' With that O'Flahertie pulled a heart-shaped potion bottle from his pocket and flicked some of its contents onto Fual's nose.

48

To Jenny's delight, the hound ceased growling and began snuffling contentedly.

He padded off after his master, who was already pounding far across the causeway.

Jenny had resolved to keep her eyes peeled once again for mermaids, dolphins and dinosaurs during the return leg.

(And so O'Flahertie waited until she was looking behind her before shaking the contents of a stripy pink-and-white pepper pot over them both...)

But there was... no sight... of anything...

Until...

POUNd POUNDD *POUNDD-DD!*

Another mythical warrior, much smaller than Finn and a good deal uglier, was pounding up behind them on the stepping stones –gaining ground by the second!

His red hair bristled in all directions as he beat his fists on a dented tartan breastplate and roared: 'AH'LL HAVE YE, THIEF FINN McCOOL. YE'LL *NAE* ESCAPE THE MIGHTY MIGHT OF BENANDONNERRR *THIS TIME!*'

Finn stopped and turned with a face like thunder.

'*DO* something, O'Flahertie,' screeched Jenny. 'No-one must see us. Make us *invisible – NOW!*'

'It is already done, dear girl. Not an adventuress or an O'Flahertie in sight, believe me! Pure magic!'

Glancing around at herself, Jenny saw that she looked distinctly fuzzy. So did O'Flahertie.

'Oh, *thank* you!' she cried. *'Thank you!'*

Brilliant, thought Jenny. *I know when I'm invisible during this adventure. That'll come in really useful.*

'THOSE BOOKS AN' PAPERRR BELONG *TAE US,*' roared Benandonner.

Scooping up one of his lucky extra stepping stones, Finn sprinted for dry land once more and hurled it over his shoulder.

Splassss hhhhhhh!

'HAH!' bellowed Benandonner, as the boulder scudded past him and splashed harmlessly into the sea. 'YE CANNY EVEN THROW LIKE A *MAN!*'

He was so close now that Jenny could smell his stinky breath (truthfully, he wasn't *that* close, it was more that his breath was unbelievably stinky).

'FUAL, *ATTACK!*' roared Finn, turning to scoop up another spare rock. (However the hound was still under O'Flahertie's hearty potion-spell and believed everyone was great − even baddies like Benandonner − so that was the end of *that.*)

SPLASSS HHHHHH!

'MISSED AGAIN, YE HUMPTY-NUMPTY!'

Benandonner *was* getting really close now. He made a ham-fisted lunge for Fual's pouch with his meaty red fingers as Jenny and O'Flahertie ducked low and sideways on the dog's back.... and...

...the books and monks' special treated parchment began to slip out and down the wolfhound's side!

'We can't let him get my souvenir parchment, O'Flahertie,' howled Jenny, as Finn and Fual sped on towards land. 'I'll be stranded hundreds of years ago if he does! We need something to put him *off!*'

Then inspiration struck.

'Horrible Dorian's essay might do the trick,' she yelled. 'Quickly, O'Flahertie!'

Grabbing the monks' special parchment first, her guide produced the not-so-ancient bright yellow roll of paper and thrust it behind to Jenny, who threw it at Benandonner.

The stocky giant snapped up the unravelling scroll with a vengeful cackle (although with a degree of puzzlement, seeing as how it had flown out of nowhere from invisible people) and paused for a vital split second.

CRASSSSSSHHHHHHH!

This time Finn's aim rang true... smashing the causeway boulder between them and his red enemy – and leaving Benandonner stranded on a boulder.

But – oh, dear – the ancient books from the printing workshop had begun to plop into the water, one by one.

51

PLOP 💧PLOP 💧 PLOP 💧 PLOP 💧

This happened in extra-slow motion, however, allowing Jenny to watch open-mouthed as a shiny black (please note: not mythical red) snake-monster rose from the sea!

Disgusted, Benandonner jumped onto one of its humps and rode off, tossing Horrible Dorian's unfinished essay into the waves as he went.

'OCH AYE THE *NOOOO*, NESSIE! BACK TAE THE *LOUGH*, WE'LL GET HIM *NEXT TIME*!' he roared, fists and hair and breastplate bristling.

'*Dive in, Jenny, DIVE!*' O'Flahertie waved the monks' reddy-yellow parchment towards a final falling book.

Its blank pages opened wide as it hit the water...

Chapter One
Returned

The corridor Jenny landed in was long and chilly and lit by bulky fluttering white candles set deep into the thick stone walls every so often.

Close-together skinny half-doors lined it on both sides (open at the top, like in a stable) with pairs of tattered brown sandals placed neatly outside (like the partying monks wore in the forest).

It must be a monastery, thought Jenny, pulling her rucksack against her robed back with a shiver.

Still, I suppose there are worse places to end up, she consoled herself, looking around for O'Flahertie. There was no sign of him. *Hmmm.*

Jenny checked her fuzziness factor next. It had disappeared. *Drat! I'm not invisible any more.*

Then she checked the date slots on her watch. One-six-five-three. *Hmmm again.* Jenny calculated that she'd whizzed forward in slightly over double time since the parchment part with Mythical Man and the monks in 806AD.

'I worked on a poem all morning and took out a comma'

Wow, she thought. *That really was the furthest adventure ago yet, by centuries. Oh, what a din!'*

Schnaw–*HHH*–*Whhh*oooo...

SCHNAW–HH–woooooooo...

Schnnawwww–*HHHHHH WHHHH*oooooooooooo!

The open tops of the half-doors began to wobble as all kinds of snorty snores filled the chilly air.

Jenny decided to risk creeping along the long corridor towards a large (whole) door at the far end. Thankfully it was ajar, by the merest sliver, for...

Creeee–aaaaaK–*KKKKK*.

'Come in, my dear girl.' O'Flahertie beckoned wearily with an ink-stained finger without looking up. 'And shut the door, if you please.'

'What's *happened* to you?' exclaimed Jenny. 'You look *awful*!'

Then she *felt* awful for saying so, especially being so delighted to see her clever, reassuring guide again. 'I'm *sorry*, I didn't mean to be rude...'

O'Flahertie raised bleary eyes and nodded gently that he didn't mind. His face had a greener glow than earlier (though he looked much the same age).

He was sprawled at a scuffed dining table in the monks' canteen-refectory as a fat candle flickered before him. His university robe lay in a huddle on the floor and his dressy shirt was covered in inky blotches. Even his floppy hair had lost its flop.

Jenny's guide sighed as he swept a heap of broken feather quill-pens and charred scraps of yellowy-red paper onto the floor.

I hope it's not the special parchment, thought Jenny in horror. *I hope he hasn't burned my souvenir for some strange reason!*

'Have you kept my souvenir parchment safe, O'Flahertie? Is this a monastery? Where–?'

'I've been trying to write for *days*, dear girl,' he interrupted, sweeping yet more papers onto the floor and snapping shut a wrinkled book with wonderful raised gold lettering on the cover.

'I was working on the proof of one of my poems all the morning, and took out a comma. In the afternoon I put it back again. It's just not–'

STOMP–MaRCH–STOMP–MaRCH–STOPPPPP.

'MY *SOLLLDIERS*, SEARCH THIS *LLLAST* ROOM FOR TREASURE AND *KILLL* ANYONE WHO STANDS IN YOUR WAY!'

O'Flahertie steered Jenny towards a panel in the wall, urgently tapping a spot there. A hidden cupboard door obligingly popped open.

They crouched in – *whew!* – as what sounded like hundreds of soldiers (but wasn't) clattered in.

CLANK, *WHOOSH,* **DING**, **CLANK,** **BINGGG**

Jenny's heart was beating so hard and so fast she was sure the deadly raiders would hear it.

THOU HAST DONE *WELLL*, MY TRUSTY

SOLLLDIERS. THREE SACKS OF *GOLLLDEN TROVE* FOR THY *FEARLLLESS LLLEADER.*'

Thud!   THUD!   THUDDDD!

The chief plunderer's yell(ll)y voice rose higher and louder. 'NOW WHAT IS THIS *HERE*?'

Jenny's heart thudded and thumped even faster. *He's exactly outside our secret hiding place!*

Thankfully their secret hiding place remained precisely that.

It didn't take the soldiers long to ransack the room, given that it was mostly empty, apart from–

'IS THAT *GOLLLD*?' bellowed the chief plunderer. '*TAKE IT!*'

The raiders' echoing footsteps had been silent for a very *very* long time before Jenny and O'Flahertie ventured out of the hidden cupboard.

'They've stolen your book for its cover,' she whispered, aghast.

O'Flahertie appeared lost in thought. Then his eyes cleared and he straightened his spine. He pulled a tiny pink jar from a trouser pocket and showered its powdery contents onto his shirt.

The ink blots vanished and his dressy shirt immediately turned crisp-white again, even neatly tying its own bow (as if by magic). He put on his fallen gown. His hair flopped properly again.

'Always forgive your enemies; nothing annoys them so much,' remarked perked-up O'Flahertie. 'Besides, I hadn't actually *written* anything in it yet. Although, that said, I *do* want it back, as I might.'

Jenny giggled, but then remembered her burning question from earlier. 'Where's my parchment souvenir to get home, please?'

Her guide turned towards the door without answering. 'They cannot have gone far,' he proclaimed. 'Follow me.'

They tiptoed down the Schnaw-*HHH*-*WOOOO* corridor – the monks were still sleeping in noisy peace, thank goodness – and out of the monastery, into a wood, out the other side, raced a bit further on still, and a bit more, until...

WHeeeezze... PAN-TTTTT... WHEEE-*ZZZZZE!*

Jenny had never run so far or so fast before and *could not believe* O'Flahertie wasn't out of breath.

'Let... me...' she gasped. '*Let...*'

'Don't worry, dear girl; we're there.'

And they were.

Once she got her breath back enough to look, Jenny could see the plundering soldiers in the near distance.

Moonlight bounced off their strange sticky-outy helmets, which included weird metal earflaps into the bargain.

Jenny and O'Flahertie inched close enough to

hear the men gloating over jewel-encrusted crosses, golden chalices and gilded goblets spread out under the silvery stars.

Despite being judged by its cover, the rumpled book lay dull and ignored beside all this enticing glittery stuff.

The soldiers began to suck up to a wispy-haired chap with cold-fish eyes and a huge hairy wart nestling under his thin cruel lips.

(Jenny reckoned he had to be the chief plunderer, although he didn't exactly *look* like one.)

According to them, he was a completely amazing leader and they absolutely couldn't do *any* of their brilliant village-pillaging and farm-burning stuff without his super-fantastic orders.

They used all kinds of old-fashioned roundabout language to say so, you understand, but that was the rotten gist of it.

'Can you make us invisible again, O'Flahertie?' asked Jenny. 'Please?'

'No, no. Not a bit of it, dear girl. This part is entirely up to you.'

Jenny bit her lip. 'But don't you have any more potions or spells or something? Otherwise how will we get the book back?'

'Do *you* have any ideas?' replied O'Flahertie, with a pointed look at Jenny's bulging backpack. 'I have, after all, helped a great deal thus far in your escapades – including saving the monks' parchment for you – and am feeling rather worn out.'

With that, he lounged low against a tree, closed his eyes and swiped several times at his brow in a most theatrical manner.

'All great ideas are dangerous,' added Jenny's guide for good measure. 'Remember that. Often you need not do things by the – ahem – *book*.'

Oh! thought Jenny. *Yes, I can use…*

'Here's the plan, O'Flahertie,' she said briskly, opening her rucksack and taking charge.

Using her university gown as a cover, Jenny crept into the campsite.

Her cunning plan was to swop O'Flahertie's book for the one Risky Self had made her take from the monks' workshop much, much, *much* earlier on.

(Stealing was totally out of character for Jenny, you'll appreciate, but Risky had convinced her to swipe an extra souvenir for Jeremiah Gnome, just in case, and she had gone along with that.)

During their boasting-stroke-flattery sessions the soldiers had quaffed gallons of smelly ale. Most of them nodded off where they sat, heads lolling. Chief Plunderer slept on his side among them, snuffling contentedly as he sucked his thumb.

I've done it! Jenny triumphantly slid the wrinkled book into her rucksack and slipped it on frontways as she crawled backwards towards safer ground.

Then two things happened at once: (a) a full-on moonbeam lit up her huddled shape like a spotlight, and (b) Chief Plunderer woke with a disturbed yelp and sat up, rubbing his eyes and staring right at her!

Aaaarrrrghhhhh! roared Jenny in her head, standing bolt upright and hoping the element of surprise would buy her some running time.

'APPREHEND THE INTRUDER!'

She fled towards the tree where O'Flahertie was waiting, hoping frantically that he had something up his sleeve – because *she* certainly hadn't.

'Up here!' Her guide was perched on a stout branch, wildly flapping his arms as his gown ballooned with air. 'Flap, Jenny. *Flap*!'

The soldiers were already in hot pursuit, although thankfully a groggy one at best.

Jenny frantically flap-flapped and flap-flapped.

O'Flahertie leaped gracefully from the tree, swooping towards her with a whoosh of welcome air which filled her robe.

In a trice the flapping pair were airborne, silhouetted against a full (and in Jenny's case, recently cruel) moon as Chief Plunderer and his nasty soldiers shook their fists and shouted helplessly behind.

Then... 'DUFFFFFFF-*UUURGGHHHH!*'

'Oh... O'Flahertie – are you *ALL RIGHT?*'

Jenny's guide had thudded into the gable of a ruined cottage!

She flapped down. He was lying in a smelly puddle.

'Nothing serious, dear girl,' he assured her, rubbing his head with a slight groan. 'It serves me right for not paying attention.'

Then, thoughtfully perusing the night sky, he remarked: 'We are all in the gutter, but some of us are looking at the stars.'

Jenny didn't understand that – but knowing O'Flahertie it was definitely worth thinking about.

She added it to the growing list of things and people and sayings to look up after she got home.

As they flew off into the starry sky, Jenny's watch clicked and whirred...

A rosy dawn was breaking as Jenny and her guide flapped towards a sleepy city.

'It's the spike thingy where I started off this adventure,' she exclaimed. 'At least I *think* it is...'

For, instead of silvery metal, the spire appeared

to be made of green jelly this time. *And* it was wobble-waving like crazy in the teeniest of breezes.

'*Why-?*'

'Pay attention, dear girl,' instructed O'Flahertie. 'It's our final descent.'

As the ivy-covered university buildings from before (or perhaps later?) in the adventure loomed close, Jenny gazed down at the bell tower.

'Oh! *Why-?*'

'Watch where you're going, m'dear. This part is always tricky. *Oooops!*'

The topmost bobble of the campanile – also now entirely built from green jelly – was quivering wildly as he tried to land!

In the end O'Flahertie boinged and slithered down one side it, tumbling onto the grass.

Jenny hovered, taking time to check her watch. It had moved by eight years from the monastery-stroke-plunderers part; they were in 1661. *Hmmm.*

She decided not to copy O'Flahertie's squelchy arrival, and glided gracefully onto the grass nearby.

Dad always says it's better to cut to the chase anyway, she thought.

'WHO GOES *THERE?*'

A lanky man in clanking armour appeared at the edge of the quadrangle-square as Jenny and O'Flahertie rose to their feet.

'I GUARD THIS *LEARNED PLACE!*' he roared,

running towards the pair. (**Clank, clank!**) 'HALT, *INTRUDERS!*'

'The book, if you please.' O'Flahertie thrust the monks' treated parchment at Jenny, who was already snapping open her rucksack to get the book.

O'Flahertie opened it on the grass while Jenny hastily stowed the parchment in her backpack.

'Dive in while I distract him,' he instructed. 'Now, I may not reach the book before the guard, so if this is goodbye, m'dear...'

What am I going to do? thought Jenny, tears welling in her eyes. *What if he's kil–?*

Do as he says, snapped Risky Self. *Quickly!*

Yoooou have nooo choooice, hooted Sensible Self.

O'Flahertie was already swoop-flapping at the bewildered guard, for all the world like a large black bat (except for his unearthly green glow, that was).

Jenny breathed a deep calm-down breath and got ready to dive...

64

Chapter Two

'Γhat book belongs to *US* and YE will *NOT* have it under ANY *CIRCUMSTANCES*!'

'HEAR, *HEARRRR*!'

The floor was cold under Jenny's cheek. Wherever she had ended up after diving into the ancient book, there wasn't room to sit up.

'No, *no, NO*! We are the *TRUE* MASTERS of LANGUAGE! The book has remained in thine learned university for ALMOST *TWO HUNDRED* YEARS and thou hast done *NOTHING* to restore it! It is *OUR* turn!'

'HEAR, *HEARRR*!' (At this point there was a smattering of clapping.)

Who are they? Jenny wondcred. *Where am I?*

Before doing anything else, though, she wriggled her rucksack off to check if the crisp reddy-yellow parchment scroll was still safe. It was. *Whew!*

Then, both tentatively and carefully, plus slowly for good measure, she peeked out to get her bearings.

Jenny had landed under a long purple-cushioned high-backed bench in a stately panelled room with rows of identical carved benches along three sides.

Totally covering the fourth wall was the most magnificent pipe organ imaginable.

It had cluster after cluster of orangey-golden pipes, large and small and in between, with beautiful planks of polished rosy wood top and bottom, left and right, separating the clusters.

The largest-of-all pipe, in the exact centre of everything, disappeared into the ornate ceiling.

Jenny was almost as impressed as by the awesome library back (or was it forward?) in 1871.

She looked at her watch to see when now was.

One-eight-five-three. Hmmm, 1853. So eighteen years earlier than when I started off in this adventure with O'Flahertie at the university.

She crawled out and peeked through a hole in the carved bench in front.

Windy insults and blustery put-downs continued to whirl between the warring sides in the heated debate over whatever book or other it was.

There was no sign of O'Flahertie. *Oh, pleeease don't let that horrible guard have got him*, pleaded Jenny in her head. *Pleeeeeease!*

The clamour from the debaters was rising. There were ten in total. Five at one end of a polished table glowed greenly; five at the other shimmered with a ghostly blue hue (one of these blinked his alive colour every so often, but more about that later).

As the morning sun winked through the grand hall's criss-cross window, Jenny glimpsed a *very* familiar stone bell tower – this time with lop-sided scaffolding all around the bobbled top.

Two of the topmost statues wore shiny yellow builders' hard hats at jaunty angles.

Oh, she thought grumpily, even though the cheeky hats *were* funny and normally Jenny would have laughed (or at least grinned) at something so out of place and time like that.

She scowled instead. *I'm back at boring old here again instead of somewhere new. Blast! And the bell tower has been built now so it's not green. It wasn't hard to figure that out. Big deal!*

She checked her fuzziness factor, although not hopefully so. *No, I'm not invisible. For goodness sake!*

Jenny was feeling fed up and sorry for herself, already sorely missing O'Flahertie's solid presence and witty remarks.

Thanks to him she had the special parchment (tick), but no souvenir pen.

And she hadn't a clue what Jeremiah Gnome's 'finished freedom document' was to get home again.

This was *NO* GOOD – *AT – ALL!*

Desperately hoping for inspiration, Jenny glared at the irate debaters.

They all had something noteworthy in common: a roll of paper or parchment sticking from a pocket, or tucked precariously behind one ear, or being waved about to underline a key point.

I bet they're writers, thought Jenny. *And probably famous ones. The blue ones are ghosts and the green ones haven't been born yet. That was easy-peasy to figure out, too. Big deal times two!*

The rumpled book they were arguing over sat squarely in the middle of the table, half-way between the two coloured fighting factions.

Jenny crawled underneath two benches and came up again behind the third for a better look.

It looked like the ancient tome Finn McCool had taken from the monks' workshop; the one she had rescued for O'Flahertie from the soldiers' camp; the very same one she had dived into at the jelly belfry while *he* saved her.

Beside it... and at this sight Jenny's stomach began to flutter wildly... beside it rested an elegant fountain pen, flashing red and green and blue in equal measure!

I bet that's my second souvenir! Well, I know what to try to do next, she mused. *But − where −is O'Flahertie?*

BONNNNGGGG! *BOONNNNNG!*

The campanile bell rang so loudly that the yellow hard hats fell off the statues.

It alarmed the bickering writers into silence.

'Tis the nonce fer to deliciate in tyme of hushe,' intoned one of the older-looking blue-hues, nodding wisely as he gazed all around the table for approval.

He had mournful droopy eyes and an equally droopy beard. A dark scarf in fine wool was wrapped around his head like an uneven wide bandage.

Everyone looked puzzled, until a kind-looking man with an electric shock of flecked hair and a patterned woolly jumper to match cleared his throat and stood up in a greenly glow.

He pulled rectangular spectacles half-way down his nose to reveal deep, deep thinking eyes, before replying: 'Yes, good idea. Let us take a break.'

Droopy Eyes looked smug as everyone else murmured their relieved agreement.

'We have the hyer hond nathelees over the boke,' he added, with sneaky smile.

Ditto confounded glances all around again.

'No, you *don't* have the upper hand in this debate,' retorted Flecky Jumper sharply. 'You're *not* going to win and you're *not* getting *our book!*'

This was greeted with rapturous applause and hearty slaps on the back from his teammates.

As the clapping continued, one of them – a handsome thinker-man who also managed to look ever so slightly confused – put his hands over his ears and grimaced.

'I'd like some peace – *right now*,' he entreated loudly, plucking at his bowtie (and pulling his glasses' chain when he wasn't doing that).

'I've been waiting for *ages* for what *I* want,' added his greenly neighbour, scrubbing at his spiky hair in frustration. 'Waiting... *waiting... WAITING!*'

Jenny gasped. *I've never seen a man with so many craggy wrinkles, even Grandad!* she thought.

Her mood had improved considerably during this welcome breather from hanging on for dear life inside jiggling trees and leaping onto giant dogs.

So much so that Jenny was making a mental list of who to find out about after she got home...

Hmmm... Finn McCool, his dog, the monks on both sides of the sea, the books, Horrible Dorian, the snake monster thingy − and of course dear O'Flahertie...

And I'll try to look up these writers as well, she added to herself. *Some of them do seem familiar...*

A portly blue chap in a curly wig with even curlier cartoon-dog ears attached rose unsteadily to his feet.

Everyone groaned. Even the campanile's bell let rip a rapid series of irritated-sounding bongs.

'I am yourrr lexicographerrr and tonguepad,' he began loudly and (but only to him) importantly.

His jowly chops quivered as he struggled with both podgy hands to open a colossal book, the word 'Dictionary' printed on its cover in silvery lettering.

'Thus therrre should be no consterrrnation or brrrabbling about the vanquisherrr of this debate, the merrritable individual on whom this grrrand

70

prrrize will be bestowed... tis *I!*' thundered Jowly Chops, pointing greedily to the fountain pen.

Naturally enough Jenny couldn't understand his odder words, but she reckoned she'd got the gist (as in: the pen was for the best individual debater and Jowly Chops had his beady eye firmly on it).

Toot! TOOT-ETTY! Toot! *TOOT!*

The tiniest pipes on the majestic organ began to toot in turn with hot air as urgent pleas for the long-winded speaker to be quiet rose in harmony from all sides.

Then... *consternation!*

The colourful pen rose into the air with a jiggle, its shiny nib making extravagant sweeps in the air.

Jenny's heart flipped as she realised it was spelling out some very familiar letters in puffs of green and red and blue air: J-E-N-N-Y

With several jabs towards the grand chamber's window, it puffed next: L-O-O-K --->

Clouds obligingly scudded in front of the sun, allowing Jenny to spot something very promising indeed.

It was a green glow and a swish of black on the bell tower's scaffolding...

Chapter Two
With Bells On

Jenny stared steadily and quietly out of the window as the befuddled writers ran here, there and everywhere, grabbing at the sweeping pen.

Could the glow possibly be O'Flahertie clinging to the wonky scaffolding?

But the sun blazed again and that was that.

An enormous black bat wheeled away from the all-too-familiar belfry.

Jenny's spirits sank. *Why did the pen tell me look out?* she wondered. *Is it definitely my second souvenir?*

It puffed again: **Y-E-S!**

Then: **WHOOOSH.... FLAP-FLAPPETY-FLAP-FLAP!**

The enormous bat had whooshed down through the organ's central pipe and was flapping around the stately hall!

Well, if the writers were befuddled before, now they were flabbergasted and flummoxed as well.

After an oddly graceful dance in the air with the

'I am the KING of VERSE and thou will never be, Sir'

jiggling fountain pen, the bat landed on the shoulder of a stout fellow whose slicked-back hair glinted ginger through his green glow.

He was clad in a smart three-piece suit with a golden watch chain looping across the waistcoat.

This greenly-stroke-ginger-haired man swatted at the bat, although in a friendly way, it must be said.

It brushed gently against his bushy beard a few times and then perched upon the top of his head for ages before flying off.

Ginger Man gasped. 'Eureka!' he thundered, before running over to the debating table and scribbling fiercely.

'Psssst, my dear. *Pssst!*'

'Oh – O'Flahertie! Where did *you* come from?' Jenny was so glad to see her witty guide she almost cried (before she remembered her brave adventuress status, that was, and didn't do anything of the sort).

'*Oh!*' she whispered. 'Were *you* the...?'

O'Flahertie nodded his green face, with the merest flap of his black university robes. 'You'll seldom see a *real* bat in the daytime, dear girl.'

And to think I thought he couldn't do magic, thought Jenny. *He's brilliant at it!*

Together they peered through the carved bench.

The writers had given up trying to catch the magic pen. It hovered above the wrinkled book, tantalisingly out of reach, still flashing blue, green and red.

Peace had broken out (for now).

Bowtie Man was telling Spiky Hair about a magic spell he could perform to give people fame and fortune – and insisting that Spiky should wait no longer for his well-deserved success.

'As long as I can get it *exactly* right,' he added.

Spiky Hair looked extremely doubtful as Bowtie Man gurgled and spluttered for ages, waving an invisible magic wand.

'Indeed happy days will not be long coming,' predicted Bowtie. 'Your endgame is... waiting... Like my longed-for peace, it comes dropping slow.'

Droopy Eyes was talking non-stop to a man on the opposing team who had a bristly moustache and was sporting a stylish suit with a stripy tie.

And (bizarre as that might seem) Stripy Tie seemed to be hanging onto his every word.

'They say they don't understand *me* either,' lamented Stripy when Droopy paused for breath. 'But my talent is, in fact, already in full bloom.'

His piercing eyes behind small thick rounded glasses beamed with delight at his new friend; he frequently doffed his crooked felt hat to Droopy in pure appreciation.

(Jenny reckoned some of Droopy's blue remarks were quite cheeky, judging by his wicked expression and sly winks – and especially the way he lowered his voice to a whisper each time.)

'Oh, woe is me / Oh, mis-er-ee,' moaned the chap flashing an alive colour in between his blue hue. 'It cuts me deep, this aged thorn / Would that I were never born.'

'What's wrong with *him*, O'Flahertie?'

'He's out of this world, m'dear. He shuffled off this mortal coil... let me see, three years ago now– but to this very day he can't get over it.'

'Ah,' replied Jenny. 'That explains why he's still so flashy.'

'You're *smiling*, O'Flahertie!' she exclaimed next. 'I don't think I've seen you smile before.'

'Well, I do know the importance of being earnest,' replied her guide with a wide grin. 'However I *am* tempted to smile at this fascinating fiasco. And the only way to get rid of a temptation is to yield to it.'

Jenny grinned back. *O'Flahertie has some brilliant expressions,* she thought. *I really must try to remember them all and look them up when I get home.*

'Now, we *will* get your souvenir pen, dear girl, but bear with me a little longer. My own business always bores me to death; I prefer other people's.'

And, because O'Flahertie was enjoying himself so much, Jenny was perfectly happy to do just that.

(And besides, although she didn't understand

absolutely everything in this part of the adventure, Jenny was finding the ridiculous antics of the probably-famous writers quite entertaining.)

(Not to mention enjoying the aforementioned welcome rest from running away from plundering soldiers etc.)

Although supposedly on the same side, the final two blue debaters sat facing nose-to-nose, looking daggers at one another.

One had deeply intelligent eyes, a lush moustache and a thin shadowy beard. Straggly locks flowing down his back made his disappearing hairline even more noticeable.

The other chap had secretive eyes, curly auburn-blue hair and a short beard that was sharply pointy. He was wearing a white neck ruff which reminded

Jenny of a dog being treated for fleas.

And *hmmm*, now that Jenny was eyeing Pointy Beard this closely...

'I think I met him in another adventure,' she informed O'Flahertie, pointing to Pointy.

Her guide smiled broadly again. 'Perhaps...'

Pointy Beard was taunting Straggly Locks about the delightful day he had been knighted by an equally delightful queen.

At this, Straggly Locks gritted his teeth and

squeezed his roll of parchment so tightly that his blue knuckles actually turned white.

'Thy poems are *doggerel*,' muttered Straggly. '*I am a true wordsmith and yet such a deserved honour was never bestowed upon* me!'

Pointy Beard was determined to rub it in. 'And for ye olde ceremony at the palace I recited my delightful rhyme to Her Majesty.

'Ah-hah-HAH-*HEMMM*.'

(*Oh no*, thought Jenny. *Pointy's poem will be truly awful. I'm certain I've heard it before...*)

O'Flahertie's shoulders shook as he chortled with mirth.

'I WOND-*DERED* lovely as a *CLOWN*–!' bellowed Pointy.

'AaaaaHH*HHH!*' yelled Flashing Chap, blinking his alive colour more and more vividly with every ear-splitting syllable. 'That is *my* poem thou art ruining. *DESIST*, imposter!'

'Perrrmit me, beneficent gentlemen, to returrrn to the weighty matterrr in hand...'

Dictionary-yawn Jowly Chops was determined to reopen the literary argument for the blue team so he could be awarded the prized pen as the best overall debater (assuming he was on the winning side in the first place, of course).

His wordy suggestion was met with a united front of cranky grumbles, tuts and 'not nows'.

*Splat‡ Splot‡ SPL*ATTTTT*‡*

The magic fountain pen began to flick madly, covering Jowly with splodges of ink as the other debaters ran helter-skelter for shelter.

However the pen wasn't taking any prisoners.

After nodding twice shyly to Speckly Jumper and puffing G-E-N-I-U-S into the air in green letters – turning a respectful black as it did so – it then squirted all the other writers as well!

During the chaos Ginger Man ran amok flapping like a bat and trying to bite people in the neck almost like... almost like a *vampire* (thankfully he never got close enough to anyone to succeed).

Even while they were ducking and diving from the ink blots, Pointy Beard continued to ridicule Straggly Locks.

He began blowing and spitting in his face, making piggy noises and taunting: 'I'll *huff* and I'll PUFF and I'll *BLOW* thy house *DOWN!*'

Straggly turned bluer and bluer with anger and frustration – until a purple patch appeared on each cheek.

At which point he whipped a jewelled sword from beneath his swingy cape and swung it at Pointy Beard, who sharply retaliated with his.

Clanggggg! Clanggg! CLANGGG!

The duelling pair clanged around the stately

debating hall as everyone else raced out of their way.

The pen flew over to the window, flashing its colours and wobbling (almost as if it were laughing).

'STOP!' implored Speckly Jumper. 'The *PEN* is mightier than the SWORD! *STOP!*'

However his wise words fell on deaf ears.

'I have *HATED* THEE for SCORES of *YEARS!*' bawled Straggly.

'Measure for measure, I am the *KING* of VERSE,' jeered Pointy, striking Straggly where it hurt. 'And thou will *NEVER* be, Sir!'

By now O'Flahertie was rolling around on the floor, clutching his splitting sides.

And Jenny was giggling just as much at her guide as the ludicrous carry-on of the probably-important writers.

'A man cannot be too careful in the choice of his enemies,' he guffawed, standing up and dusting himself off. 'And these two gentlemen –' (CHortLe, guFFaW) – 'are clearly demonstrating my point.

'Come along, dear girl. – (guFFaW, CHortLe) – Most unfortunately, it is high time we moved on.'

'Who won the debate in the end, do you know?' asked Jenny, who always liked loose ends tied up.

'You must wait and see, m'dear. Time will tell.'

All other eyes were on the swashbuckling pair as Jenny and her guide skirted the stately debating chamber and made for the grand pipe organ.

O'Flahertie pumped its foot pedal.

Hot air blasted down from the huge central pipe.

Their robes billowed. In a trice the pair were flapping above the mayhem.

'LOOK *UP!*' roared Jowly Chops. 'WHAT malagrrrugrrrous complexity is *THIS*?'

Straggly Locks and Pointy Beard dropped their swords with a **CLANG-CLANG** as a perplexed silence fell.

Jenny flapped towards the precious magic pen and made a grab for it. It deftly dodged her swiping fingers several times before she managed to grasp it. *Whew!*

The cover of the rumpled book on the debating table flipped open. Its pages rustled.

Jowly Chops rushed towards it, eyes wide with... well, with whatever impossibly long-drawn-out word he would use instead of 'shock'.

With no time to turn and dive in, Jenny steadied herself directly above the book, took a deep breath, stopped flapping – and plummeted in feet first...

Chapter Three

GPO

CLANGGGG...! CLANGGGG...! CLANNGGG...!
Door after door after door clanged shut amid
a powerful jumble of howls and grunts and
bawls and groans.

'Let us *out*! We're *INNOCENT!*'

'We *shouldn't* be *LOCKED UP* in HERE!'

Jenny didn't like the sound of *this*. She had ended
up squeezed into a tiny alcove somewhere. Her heart
was pounding and her mouth was dry.

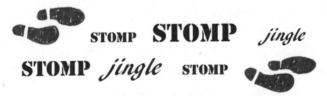 STOMP **STOMP** *jingle* **STOMP** *jingle* STOMP

The heavy jingling footsteps faded. Jenny
breathed a silent sigh of relief and studied her
watch. The date squares read one-nine-one-six.

She peeked out from the alcove, which was in a
high vaulted hallway (perhaps better described as a
huge foyer like in a grand theatre, given that it was
truly huge and very grand), with rows of black doors

'The pair raced towards the prison's soaring main door'

all around on three floors. On the topmost floor, the fourth, the black doors nestled behind large arches.

An ornate wrought-iron staircase with cut-out twiddly bits sliced up through the middle of the hallway-stroke-foyer like an arrow.

It rested on equally ornate metal walkways to the left and right on each level – like footbridges over a railway – which connected everything to everywhere.

Yet more swirly iron bits looped out from beside the door arches on the top floor, all joining together in an even more complicated swirl under the centre of a curved glass roof.

If this building wasn't a miserable old prison, thought Jenny, risking a longer peek from her hiding place – *it would be really beautiful.*

The rebellious pleas continued. Flat hands slapped on doors. Faces squashed up against bars.

'Set us *FREE* – we're *innocent!*'

'... don't DESERVE to be locked *up!*'

'... *fighters* for *FREEDOM!*'

Jenny tried not to panic as the din ebbed and flowed around her. *Oh, O'Flahertie? Where ARE you?* she wailed in her head, pulling her gown tightly around her with a shudder.

'Pssst!'

The prisoner in the cell beside the alcove had

spotted Jenny during her last longer look! Her heart dipped and speeded up all at once.

I need to get out of here – and fast, before they all see me!

'Dear girl, *pssssst! It's me!*'

Oh – O'Flahertie! Jenny was overjoyed. She wanted to rush over to him, but it was far too risky.

Instead she did a quick around-the-corner wave from her alcove... hoping nobody else spotted it.

'*Get me out, m'dear!*' he hiss-whispered.

Jenny dug deep for ideas but came up empty.

Surely O'Flahertie can magic himself out through the door? she thought. *It can't be that difficult.*

'I have no potions *left* and can only use my bat signal *once*,' louder-hissed Jenny's guide, almost as if he had read her mind. 'You must get a *key*.'

Jenny gulped. She really didn't fancy trying to follow the prison guard and steal his jingling keys – assuming she could pull that off in the first place – never mind the tricky task of figuring out which of the bunch would open O'Flahertie's door.

And even if she *did* manage all that, what if the other prisoners heard the door opening and shouted at Jenny to release them? The stomping guard would return for sure and they would *both* be caught.

This was no good AT *ALL*.

You have to ris– Risky Self screeched up and began giving orders, as per usual.

Hang on a moooment, interrupted Sensible Self. *Sooometimes it can be better tooo wait...*

So Jenny stuck out her arm once more and gave (what she hoped was) a low-key yet reassuring thumbs-up around towards O'Flahertie. She began frantically racking her brains again, until....

Her pocket began to tingle.

The magic pen!

Jenny drew out the precious souvenir.

For an agonising few moments it remained black and flat in her palm.

Come on, she pleaded, *pleeease show me how to set O'Flahertie free!*

Then slowly – very *very* slowly indeed – the pen began to flash its true colours.

BLiNK, red; bLiNK, greeN; bLiNK, bLue

Gradually the nib changed shape, growing fatter and wider and adding different-shaped bits... until it was exactly like an old key!

Brilliant, thought Jenny. *Now I just have to let him out without anyone else noticing.*

The clamour grew as the protesting prisoners began dinging the bars with pots and kicking at the doors.

Jenny crouched low and sidled sideways towards O'Flahertie's cell, urgently waving the magical pen-stroke-key up at his dear frazzled face (which, she noticed immediately, despite everything else that was going on, wasn't green any more, like before. *Hmmm*).

In a trice the lock was unlocked.

Together the pair raced towards the prison's soaring main door. It was so heavy it took several more trices to get it open, but then they were free...

Well, not *quite*...

They found themselves in a stony courtyard with high, high walls. Even in the bright afternoon sunshine, this was a chilly, gloomy place.

A shimmery black hangman's gallows clanked and creaked. The wall behind it was pock-marked with scores and scores of bullet holes.

Jenny shivered. O'Flahertie shuddered.

They raced to a gate in the furthest corner, where thankfully the pen-key obliged again.

In another trice they were standing on a wide hilly street lined with low higgledy-piggledy cottages.

'Which way now, O'Flahertie?' asked Jenny.

'Pardon?' he replied distractedly.

Jenny's guide had paused to shoot a disgusted glare at a sign on the prison wall reading 'Gaol'.

'Society often forgives the criminal; it never forgives the dreamer,' he spat bitterly.

Then, after a defiant toss of his floppy hair, he replied in his normal calm tone: 'To the right, m'dear; to the right.'

Bang! BANG! *Bangety-bang.*

Bullets whizzed past as the pair raced down the street. O'Flahertie flap-flapped, so Jenny did, too – but with several cruel **bang-bangs** their chance of flight was shot to ribbons.

'Quick – this way,' ordered O'Flahertie.

He sped down a narrow lane, around a couple of corners and then deftly steered Jenny through a chink in the middle of an enormous black gate with a gold harp painted on it.

They ducked into a (thankfully empty) little hut just inside it for Jenny to catch her breath.

O'Flahertie hummed a perky tune while he waited; then, spotting in-and-out bullet holes and several tears in his flowing gown, tutted for ages.

'*Poooh!*' gasped Jenny, as soon as she possibly could. 'What's that *smell? It's like nothing I've ever smelled before. Yuk!*'

O'Flahertie grinned. 'Are you ready to move on, dear girl? We need to get ahead.'

Jenny nodded, pinching her nose and very sorry she had *ever* thought the bell tower was boring.

She had certainly never imagined that seeing more of the sights in wherever city this was might be done down the barrel of a rifle!

'I think we'll go over and across here, dear girl, and then over there another little bit.' O'Flahertie seemed totally relaxed about everything now.

They were in a giant factory; that much was clear.

Steam puffed around old red-bricked buildings with gracious arched windows and elegant chimneys.

It hissed around low grey flat blocky ones and glistening metal vats as large as houses.

It huffed around a stone tower shaped like an upside-down ice-cream cone, with a green splodge on the top (which had once been copper).

People rushed about here and there, all looking far too busy and important to notice Jenny and her guide.

'Ah yes, we shall take another breather in here,' he instructed, sauntering down an uneven flight of worn-down-in-the-middle stone steps.

CreeeaKKKKK (fizz...fizz...)

They entered a cellar filled with fizzing vats and high rows of ancient barrels stored on their sides.

The indescribable pong was even stronger in there, but at least it appeared to be empty... and at this stage Jenny was grateful for just about anything that didn't involve gunfire (or spooky courtyards with gallows, for that matter).

She unpinched her nose for a moment. 'What's the fighting about, O'Flahertie? Why were people shooting in the street?'

'Ah, it's a very long story, m'dear. Centuries and centuries long, in fact. Suffice to say that where we're at doesn't want to be part of somewhere else any more, if indeed it ever did – and the rebels will fight to the death for independence in the end.'

'I'm not sure that I...?' Jenny couldn't make sense of O'Flahertie's cryptic explanation.

'Ah, I am so clever that sometimes I don't understand a single word I am saying,' he replied, giving himself an approving pat on the back.

I'll have to look up the history when I get home, like all the other stuff, decided Jenny, *once I know when it happened.*

She checked her watch again. It was still 1916. *Hmmm.*

Jenny looked closely at O'Flahertie's face.

How odd, she thought.

During his glowing green times in their adventures to date her guide had remained as young-looking as his real student self back in 1871.

Now that he was his alive colour again, however,

he looked about Dad or Uncle Donal's age – exactly like the very first time Jenny had seen him shimmering blue in the sky beside the spire thingy.

But – she did a quick headcount – *this is 45 years later than 1871. That can't be right. Surely he should look much older now?*

It was a pretty trivial matter in the grand scheme of things, she knew, but – insofar as it was possible – Jenny did like things to add up, even in her crazy magic adventures.

'Shouldn't you be...?' she began carefully. 'Shouldn't you look – well, *older?*'

'Oh, I'm way beyond wrinkles, my dear girl,' he replied with a wry smile. 'In fact, I should really be a ghastly blue these past sixteen years, but I've decided that *that* colour really doesn't suit me for this part.

'This escapade is bubbling along nicely and I want to look and feel my best, you understand. I certainly don't want to be feeling blue. Now, let us go, m'dear.'

Jenny hesitated. She didn't particularly like it in the smelly cellar, but at least they weren't in the line of fire in there.

We can't even fly any more, she fretted, taking off her useless robe and putting it into her backpack.

Gooo ooout–

Oh, be quiet, Sensible Self!

Jenny cleared her throat. And then decided, sensibly, that she had better get on with things.

If even Sensible Self is in favour of going out again, I really should, she reasoned. *But I'm not doing it unless we're invisible. And that's that.*

'I'm not going out there unless we're invisible and that's that,' she told O'Flahertie firmly. 'Are you certain you don't have any magic potions left?'

'No, dear girl. Not a single drop.'

The exact moment Jenny wondered if the magic pen would help, it jiggled in her pocket and made a rude squirting noise.

She placed the souvenir (now pen-shaped again) in the palm of her hand. As she gazed at it, a drop of ink ran towards her thumb....

...which all at once appeared fuzzy...

The pen had somehow filled with invisible ink!

She quickly sprinkled O'Flahertie's feet first, and then her own, working upwards on both of them until there was nothing solid left to see except their heads.

Sprinkle... sprink... spr.. ink... spr–

'Oh *no!*' exclaimed Jenny. 'It's run out!'

Even unflappable O'Flahertie seemed dismayed.

Jenny had a feeling the adventure might be coming to a head and the freedom document wasn't far off – but how on earth could they search for it attracting attention like bobbing targets at a funfair?

She stamped her foot. 'We can't go out like *this*, O'Flahertie. Are you *sure* you don't have any potions? Or spells? Are you *absolutely certain*?'

Shaking his head, Jenny's guide leaned back against a bank of sideways wooden barrels, looking thoroughly fed up. Jenny joined him.

'I'm stumped, dear girl,' he replied, scratching his smooth chin.

'So am I,' added Jenny, tossing her long hair.

It would have looked bizarre in the very extreme had anybody walked in and spotted the two talking heads side by side.

Suddenly, with a judder and several fizzes, a wooden barrel above them began to turn pink.

Fizz...fizz...FIZZZ

'*Ugh!*' cried Jenny.

The contents fizzed out, coating them in froth.

This is going from bad to worse, thought Jenny, her temper starting to bubble... until she realised that O'Flahertie's puzzled head had gone fuzzy.

The froth had done the trick.

'Let's go,' she declared, with far more confidence than she actually felt.

Chapter Three
Unseen

They halted at a wide crossroads with two magnificent grey cathedrals either way you looked. The stony up-and-down black tower of a castle loomed right behind the one to the right.

'Which... way... *now*, O'Flahertie?' panted Jenny, bending over to catch her breath and brush the last bits of froth from her clothes (sadly there was nothing she could do about the pong).

'To the right is right, dear girl,' he replied, between carefree whistles. 'And do please take your time to recover. We have been running for at least ten minutes, after all, and it is rather warm this afternoon.'

'*Thanks,*' wheezed Jenny, '*but I'm fine to go on.*'

'The only thing to do with good advice is pass it on,' he replied modestly. 'It is never any use to oneself.'

As they jogged towards the pointier of the grey cathedrals, this one set in lush, landscaped gardens,

'...*summons her children to her flag and strikes for her freedom*'

Jenny's heart thumped even more wildly. In truth, given the close gunfire call in the street earlier, she was having *very* serious doubts about this adventure.

Being invisible is a big help, but it mightn't save us if we're caught up in crossfire again, she fretted.

Hooow will you get hooome if you don't find the freedooom dooocument?

I know you're right, Sensible Self, replied Jenny slowly in her head, *but...*

Risky rowed in, in a soft voice Jenny had never heard before. *Yes, it's scary – but you'll just have to trust O'Flahertie, and yourself, and get on with it.*

They had reached the cathedral's gardens.

Jenny's guide signalled with a flat hand to stop.

She stared up at him with worried eyes, hoping for reassurance.

He smiled warmly. 'All will be well, dear girl.'

'Thank you, O'Flahertie,' replied Jenny quietly – still anxious, but less so.

'Not at all, m'dear.' O'Flahertie opened the gate. 'Always happy to oblige when consolation is required. One should always play fairly when one has the winning cards. I shall enter first; follow me.'

Clusters of men, young and old and somewhere in between, were crouched behind a garden bench there or a clump of bushes here.

They were dressed in a motley mix of dark jackets and light shirts, ties and not, long and short trousers, flat caps and felt hats. They had rifles under their arms or on the ground beside them. They were poring over maps and whispering in furious rebellious voices.

They must be the rebels who don't want to be part of somewhere else, deduced Jenny (quite correctly).

MARCH, MARCH, MARCHY-MARCH-MARCH.

The rebels fell silent and grabbed for their rifles as a platoon of stiff soldiers in black uniforms approached the cathedral from the faraway side.

'HALT!' The marching did so.

'ATTEN-SHUN!' The stiff-straight soldiers raised their rifles and advanced towards the gardens.

The rebels remained crouching as...

CRACK–Rat–a–tat–CRACK–crack–CRACK!

Crack after crack after *crack* rang out.

Jenny and O'Flahertie fled through an arch in the cathedral gardens and into the castle grounds.

Racing across a cobblestone yard, O'Flahertie scooted though the nearest open door with Jenny hot on his heels.

Whew! she thought. *That was close – again! Goodness, I hope nobody was killed. But they probably...*

Taking several deep, deep calm-down breaths, Jenny tried not to think about *that* as best she could.

The pair were in a splendid panelled boardroom. Around its gleaming table sat a group of women wearing various smart tweed outfits.

(On seeing them Jenny almost panicked, but then remembered about being fuzzily invisible and stood her ground with O'Flahertie just inside the door. *Whew again!*)

The women were perusing crisp maps rolled out in rows with coloured pins, and pointing out the exact detail of what was to be done where in order to defeat the soldiers.

They took it in turns to speak calmly, and they all clearly looked up to a woman sitting regally at the head of the table.

She nodded respectful approval at every rebellious suggestion, but although she sometimes smiled with her eyes the rest of her face remained sad and wistful.

'The document is to be printed–' the lady looked at her wristwatch, smoothed a stray wisp of hair back into her tidy bun and signalled for the maps to be rolled up – 'in one hour precisely. Let us proceed. There is no time to lose.'

I bet she means the freedom document that I need to touch to get home, thought Jenny. *I hope I can find it soon. I wonder who these women rebels are...*

'Who–?' she whispered in O'Flahertie's ear.

'*Shhh,* dear girl. The ladies are leaving now, so move aside from the door, if you please.'

The group left the boardroom in an orderly single file, with Jenny and O'Flahertie at the end.

MARCH, MARCH, MARCH, MARCH, MARCH...

As they marched and marched through many city streets, excited men and women and boys and girls joined behind in a gaggle.

Jenny was looking forward to getting home now. But she was also enjoying being part of this eager crowd – although some people did bump into her with surprised looks, saying faint 'Sorrys' through her and across to each other as if they couldn't quite believe how the invisible bump had happened.

O'Flahertie whistled and hummed (not at the same time, obviously), inspecting people with delight and taking it all in.

He paused frequently to make notes with a quill feather on crumpled pieces of paper against one knee or other, jogging effortlessly to catch up.

As they marched through and down yet more streets lined with shops, the afternoon sun disappeared and clouds began to gather.

The crowd's chattering grew as a tall, ugly building with a wrinkly green (but non-jelly this time) roof came into view along a swirling river.

Jenny had caught enough snatches of the chattering to realise that the freedom document was to be printed in this tall, ugly building.

Sure enough, bang on cue, there was a faint

rumble in the far distance – and the building's corrugated green roof began to vibrate.

MARCH, CHatter, CHat, SKIP, CHatter-CHat, MARCH

(RUMBLE, RUMBLE...)

'Quickly now,' ordered the wistful lady, but in a reassuring, kindly tone. 'The machines are running.'

Every single person obligingly speeded up.

Jenny and O'Flahertie weaved their way to just in behind the front marchers.

The crowd **MARCH-CHatter-RUSH-MARCHED** along the river and past several nondescript wide bridges before the women stopped beside a quaint one.

This narrow hump-backed bridge had three swirly metal arches featuring flickering gas lamps at their arched top tips.

A clean-cut man with dark hair wearing a suit and felt hat was standing in the middle of it, reading from a scroll of white paper.

Three men times two stood on either side of him as the man proclaimed in an imperious voice:

'... *summons* her children to her *flag* and strikes for her freedom... strikes for her *FREEDOM!*'

These must be the lead rebels and this is the freedom document I have to touch to get home! Jenny's heart leapt. *Great!* And *I've got my two souvenirs for Jeremiah... not like before, when I–*

Ahem-*AHEM*. '... summons her *CHILDREN* to her flag and strikes for her *FREEDOMMM...*'

After a few more rehearsals, the clean-cut lead rebel – who had stood in side profile looking towards the tall, ugly building the entire time – nodded his satisfaction.

'To the printing presses!' he roared, tucking the roll of paper under his arm.

But...

A breeze whipped up. The skies opened. Sheets and buckets and bathtubs-worth of rain fell within a matter of seconds.

And...

'Ahhhhhh*HHHHHHH*!'

The roll of paper had turned into a sodden lump!

A complete and outright and shocked and speechless silence fell like dominoes as the drenched people realised what had happened.

RUMBLE, RUMBLE, RUMBLE...

The printing presses in the tall, ugly building rumbled harder in the nearer distance as the bucketing rain relented to a heavy drizzle.

This was a grotesque, unbelievable, bizarre and unprecedented *disaster!*

The rebel women joined the men on the quaint bridge in a busy huddle to figure out a Plan B.

The crowd continued to gasp and gabble, too shocked even to think of looking for shelter.

Even before the special parchment began to crackle in her rucksack, however, Jenny knew she could have the answer. She pulled out the reddy-yellow roll, noting with interest that it appeared fully and non-fuzzily in mid-air.

(Often when Jenny became invisible in her adventures everything and everyone she touched became so as well; she just needed to check which way it worked in each one.)

Thankfully anyone close enough to see this was far too upset to notice.

Yes! The raindrops were running smoothly down the parchment; its crispness remained totally crisp.

O'Flahertie watched approvingly while Jenny drew out the magic pen.

But it remained silent and colourless in her hand. *Drat!* she thought. *It's empty, and it was only invisible ink anyway. That's no good to us now.*

'Are you *certain* you don't have any more potions, O'Flahertie?' whispered Jenny as the swaying crowd continued to sway and lament.

'Not as such, dear girl,' he replied calmly, 'but I *did* take something rather special from the monks for my own modest endeavours, after you spurred on my decision in the tree to begin endeavouring them.'

With that he produced a squat bottle, its label bearing the welcome words *'Waterproof Ink'.*

RUMBLE, RUMBLE, RUMBLE...

The printing machines rumbled faster and more insistently as the tall, ugly building's roof juddered.

With O'Flahertie's help, Jenny filled the magic pen with ink before laying her two souvenirs on the bridge beside the worried rebel-huddle.

O'Flahertie kept an elegant foot on each edge of the spread-out parchment in case it blew away while Jenny went to tap the sad-faced lady on the back.

With a surprised cry (and the faintest glimmer of a smile), she rushed over and picked up the two souvenirs.

The rain stopped. The sun shone. It was a miracle! Everything and everyone was instantly dry. Double ditto!

And, to Jenny's absolute delight, the downpour had washed away the frothy smell, but thankfully not – she had been keeping a keen eye on this since the skies opened – their invisibility factor.

RUMBLE, RUMBLE, RUMBLE...

'We have no time – you must write it on the run,' said the rebel lady to the clean-cut man.

He nodded gratefully and set off at a gallop. Everybody streamed behind them over the humped bridge (because it was so narrow this took ages, and was still happening during much of the next part).

Two of his loyal followers held the parchment on both sides as the clean-cut rebel tried to write properly – but it jiggled far too much for that.

By now the printing presses were deafening.

'We *cannot* miss our *SLOT!*' he shouted, still trying to run and write. 'We *MUST* have our proclamation *PRINTED!*'

Then Jenny had a brainwave.

She wheeled around in front and bent slightly forward so he could use her back as a sloping support to write on (this was a tricky feat on the move, but Jenny judged it to perfection).

O'Flahertie rushed in beside her to steady the fountain pen and guide the leader's hand as they sprinted together in a tight bundle alongside the river, the jabbering crowd still swelling over the picturesque bridge behind.

'Anyone can make history; only a great man can write it,' proclaimed O'Flahertie with a broad beam.

The rebel leader was writing the last word of the document as they reached the steps of the tall, ugly building, when...

Silence. The rumbling– stopped. Short.

So did everyone else.

A short stocky printer swung open the door.

'You're *late*,' he shouted, his red face getting redder and redder. 'I've turned off the *machines!*'

'Why is *he* totally red?' asked Jenny. 'Is he mythical as well, then? He's hardly a monster!'

'Ah, yes, mythical indeed, m'dear. Nobody could conceivably be as cantankerous as that in real life –

if indeed this *is* real life, or in fact based on some very odd version of it. Which it may or may not be...'

O'Flahertie's voice tailed off... but his eyes glinted with joyful mischief.

Jenny decided to figure all that out later (again).

'Well, start them up again, *right now!*' retorted the rebel, striding up the steps and in under the porch with his six loyal companions close behind.

He handed the parchment and pen to his nearest running mate for signing as the printer jiggled his pot belly, flapped annoyed hands, rolled his eyes – a *lot* – and tutted for ages.

'Oh, all *right* then,' he conceded eventually.

'Shouldn't we sign it in alphabetical order?' asked one of the other waiting rebels (quite reasonably, by Jenny's reckoning).

'Good idea, but too late,' replied his leader, taking his turn among the gathered men.

'One hour and not *one second longer*,' he ordered the cranky printer, hanging tightly to the precious parchment as the ink dried. 'And, as agreed, you must deliver it to our stronghold, where I will proclaim it.'

Trying to tug it off him, the printer rolled his red eyes again and retorted that (a) because *they* had been late, so would the *printing* be, and (b) it was *at least* a five-minute walk to the post-office stronghold and he'd have to think *very carefully* about that now, bearing in mind the aforementioned *lateness* issue.

'*We* will return and bring it back to you.' The wistful lady looked to her group for agreement.

All the other women nodded enthusiastically and chorused with one voice: '*It will be our pleasure.*'

The wistful lady looked delighted (as did Jenny, who always loved it when people became happier).

Although if this is the finished freedom document to get home, she thought, *I suppose I'd better touch it now.*

The truth was that she was very much hoping Jeremiah had meant the printed version of later on.

I want to hear the rebels proclaim their freedom, thought Jenny. *I do so hope nobody has died, though, and that it all gets sorted out really soon.*

She raised her eyebrows in a question mark to O'Flahertie, who was standing beside her with an unreadable expression on his dear, earnest face.

'If my only way to get home is this handwritten parchment, O'Flahertie, then I should probably touch it in case I don't get another chance...?'

After a long pause, he blinked several times and gave a slight nod.

Jenny pushed over to between the clean-cut man and the bad-tempered printer, who were still deep in a glaring tug-of-war over the parchment.

She gently tipped its rustly middle.

Whew! thought Jenny. *I'm still here.*

At that moment, the lead rebel let go and the printer staggered backwards, whirling upright again to slam the door in everyone's faces.

'To the post office!' bellowed the seven men as one, racing off again (but not before Jenny did something very intelligent indeed for later on).

The whooping crowed followed in yet another enthusiastic swell.

Suddenly the city street was empty of anyone to be seen.

'Shouldn't we follow them, O'Flahertie?'

'Ah, plenty of time, dear girl,' he assured her, sitting down in the porch of the tall, ugly building and taking off his damaged gown.

Shaking his head, O'Flahertie brushed flecks of invisibility froth from the robe's inside shoulders, tut-tutted a few times more over the bullet holes and tears, yawned and sighed.

'Do you know, dear girl, I have a slight headache and therefore intend to take a short nap.'

With that he began puffing into the nearest edge of his robe to make a pillow.

The poor thing responded as best it could, but flatly, it must be said, and with a tired, wheezy sigh.

'That will have to do, I suppose.' Jenny's guide snapped on an eye mask and popped in earplugs.

RUMBLE, RUMBLE, RUMBLE...

Looking up towards the renewed rumbles, Jenny

spotted a red glow from a window high in the tall, ugly building.

The surly printer was emptying a basket of paper out of the window, cackling at the top of his voice.

(CackLe, CACKLE) 'I always feel *much* better after tidying the place up!' *(CACKLE!)*

Jenny yawned, feeling a little woozy and headache-y herself.

If there's no rush I might doze off for a few moments, she thought. *It can't do any harm, and I must wait for O'Flahertie to wake up before I can go anywhere, anyway.*

Just before Jenny's eyelids drooped, she watched a roll of reddy-yellow parchment float down and nudge her dear guide on his nose.

Whereupon he pulled down his sleeping mask, looked at it – and whistled delightedly...

The Start of The End

The crisp and even sound of marching, exactly in step and precisely in time, woke Jenny with a start. She looked for her guide. He was snoozing beside her on the porch.

'Wake *up*, O'Flahertie,' she hissed into his earplugged ear, poking him on the shoulder for good measure (and checking the date: it hadn't changed). *'They're coming back for the finished freedom document!'*

'Errrr-*hummph. Oh*, oh – right you are, dear girl.' Jenny's guide removed his mask and plugs, yawned, stretched and stood up. He nudged his now-flat university robe with a respectful foot and sighed. 'Rest easy there, dear useful companion.'

A mere moment after O'Flahertie began to walk away from the porch, however, he turned back.

MARCH, MARCH, MARCHETY-MARCH, MARCH

'Actually, no,' he remarked. 'There are many things that we would throw away, if we were not afraid that others might pick them up.'

'All kinds of colourful faces began rising before Jenny's eyes'

He signalled for Jenny to put his beloved robe into her rucksack, which she duly did – tucking it in beside her own borrowed one.

MARCH, MARCHETY-MAR–

The formerly wistful woman had come up the steps and was approaching the door, a contented half-smile hovering on her lips.

Crreeeeak WHOOSH! WHeeEEeeEE SLAMMM!

A roll of bright white parchment flew past Jenny's nose and did a high loop-the-loop before bouncing down the steps. The door slammed.

The printed scroll was handed to the woman by a beaming colleague with thick curly hair tied loosely back and a circular gold brooch pinned high on one shoulder.

The former tucked it snugly under her jacket and the two ladies struck up an intense conversation as they led the way to the rebels' stronghold (wherever that was, but not far away).

'That's *definitely* the finished freedom document I need to touch to get home, isn't it, O'Flahertie?'

Her guide paused for a long moment, then nodded.

Jenny was feeling excited about hearing the freedom document being read out – they *had* saved the day to get it printed, after all. *I'll touch it straight after that and go home,* she decided.

As the group turned in from the river and onto a

wide city street, Jenny spied the green-jelly spike again, quivering against the sunny sky.

A serious commotion was coming from the building opposite the wobbling spire.

This was a magnificent place altogether, standing at least three graceful storeys tall and with an impressive six-columned porch.

(Jenny thought she could see windows peeking out behind the balcony all around the top, so that would make it three-and-a-half, she supposed.)

The group entered the building's noisy hall... well... just about.

For it was crammed with people, with barely room for more... and... suddenly the women were nowhere to be seen.

And neither was O'Flahertie! Jenny's guide had vanished into the crush as well. *Oh, no!*

Deep breaths, deep breaths, deep breaths... Jenny inhaled deeply to stop herself panicking.

This took several tries, but eventually it worked. Then...

Hang on a moment, thought Jenny, *I'm not quite as fuzzy as I was. I wonder could the invisibility potions be wearing off?*

After even more calm-down breaths, she sensibly decided to do a sight (and sound) check.

People are wearing all kinds of different clothes, so even if I become visible soon, or even if I am already, my jumper and jeans won't stand out too much, she reasoned.

Jenny decided to risk speaking to a friendly-looking fellow in jeans and a leather jacket standing jammed next to her.

Despite his greenly glow, she could make out brown hair and yellow eyeglasses.

Just as Jenny turned towards him, however, the chap began singing 'trapped in a situation you can't escape from' in an oddly high-pitched – but not unattractive, it must be said – voice.

'Hello there? He-*ll-oo*?' she said tentatively.

He smiled vaguely through Jenny and began to hum instead, and to rattle some loose change in his pocket.

While relieved to still be invisible, Jenny was seriously worried about getting home now.

'What if that man's song was a signal? she fretted. *What if* I'm *trapped here? I need to touch the freedom document and get home – right now! Oh, where's…?*

'Pssst, m'dear – up here!'

Dear, *dear* O'Flahertie was perched on a window ledge high above the hordes, drumming his heels against a smoky bullet-streaked wall and waving.

'How did you get…?' A mystified Jenny mouth-whispered the words up at her guide.

He tapped his nose knowingly and winked.

The commotion peaked – and then… it… Stopped.

Somehow enough room was cleared for the leading rebel and his six companions to enter the throng.

'Oh no!' exclaimed Jenny in horror (for all these men were now flashing faintly blue in between their alive colour). 'They must be going to be *ki*–'

'Dear *girl*, I–'

'Oh, O'Flahertie – how did you get *down*? Oh, never mind. That's not important now. Look at the colour of those brave men – this is *terrible!*'

'Indeed, it *is* terrible,' he consoled her, skilfully steering his younger charge towards a nearby (low) window sill and helping her to clamber up.

'However, you are an adventuress and thus must take some downs with the ups. That is the life you have chosen, m'dear.'

'You're right of course, O'Flahertie,' replied Jenny slowly, her voice breaking. 'I just... I just can't *bear* to think of... I need to find that freedom document and go home *right now.'*

On cue the women from earlier emerged from a huddle somewhere.

The proclamation-bringer – now wistful again, and quite understandably so – handed the roll of white paper to the rebel leader. He began inspecting it closely and murmuring under his breath.

The post office filled with even more extra people as Jenny tried to quell her upset at the fate of the seven men they had helped to sign the parchment (and quite possibly many more brave rebels, too).

'Can't we *save* them, O'Flahertie?' she whispered. 'Isn't there *anything* we can *do?*'

Her guide shook his head. 'Not in this particular instance, dear girl. But I believe you may have other opportunities in other adventures, if you please.'

Jenny cheered up slightly at this, squared her shoulders and rubbed her eyes. *It's like Risky Self always says,* she figured, *I just have to get on with it.*

Just below them a glowing green man with a 'Press' card stuck onto the top of his hat was somehow managing to use a tape recorder, a camera and a notebook all at the same time – and – was that... *could it be a clunky old mobile phone as well?*

Jenny double-triple-checked her watch. *Hmmm, still 1916. That's bizarre,* she thought. *Oh well, that reporter chap must just be way ahead of his time, simple as that.*

The busy-busy journalist was interviewing a tiny-*tiny* man who was speaking in a peculiar singsong accent.

The hair all around the interviewee's bald crown (exactly like the partying monks had had in the forest) flapped as he enthusiastically waved his green arms.

The busy journalist sighed as the man then produced a book marked 'Mine Own Marvellous Poetry' and began reading aloud from it.

'Look, O'Flahertie!' – Jenny had just spied a deep red glow rising from the crowd – 'It's Mythical Man from centuries ago; it's Finn McCool!'

After that, all kinds of famous colourful faces – some from her adventures and others not – began rising towards the rafters.

They included the aforementioned partying monks and clever Fual the wolfhound (all, sadly, a ghostly blue hue), rising from among the many, many, *many* scores of alive folk...

...and there were so very many of *them* that Jenny marvelled at how they had actually all fitted in (or did they?).

The lead rebel had finished studying the printed parchment. He cleared his throat and nodded.

'I will proclaim it *OUTSIDE!*' he boomed.

Everyone squeezed back and aside to let him stride out the door.

The outside people began cheering and clapping, realising they were going to hear the proclamation first-hand.

Everyone inside streamed outside in the leader's wake (as best they could stream, given the crush).

Jenny and O'Flahertie were swept along and out and around in the sea of people, tantalisingly close to the lead rebel at one point... but then far and beyond him – and, most importantly, Jenny's finished freedom document.

'Ahhh-hhhha-*hhhemmmm.*'

He cleared his throat

Then fell silent.

He stared at the ground.

An eerie silence spread over the city...

The Middle of The End

'What's he waiting for, O'Flahertie?' gasped Jenny, craning her neck to see what. She was most alarmed by (a) the silence, and (b) the fact that they were now so very *very* far from the document she needed to touch to get home.

'He's waiting for the mythical steps to rise,' replied O'Flahertie with a chuckle. 'It's a standing joke in this place.'

'Won't he speak until there are some, then?' squeaked Jenny, *extremely* alarmed now.

'That's about the height of it, dear girl.'

Jenny racked her brains. Mythical steps were most certainly only going to rise by magic, so...

At that, the pen jiggled in her pocket (for the brainy adventuress had thought to swipe it back amid the commotion after the seven men signed the proclamation and raced off to the post office – and a very smart move it was, too).

It was a weak jiggle, but a jiggle nonetheless.

118

Jenny whipped out the magic pen with a relieved 'Whew!'

But there weren't any flashes of brilliance from her handy souvenir this time. A drop of real ink dribbled out and stained her fingers.

The silence deepened and lengthened.

Jenny looked pleadingly at her guide.

'I don't always oblige, as you know,' he replied, 'but on this one last occasion, I suppose I might.'

Producing a red bottle marked 'STEPS' (helpfully, in the shape of steps), O'Flahertie added with a wry smile: 'Illusion is the first of all pleasures, dear girl.'

'Oh, thank you,' cried Jenny, completely grateful for his undoubtedly superb and magical guiding abilities (and sorry she had ever doubted them all those centuries ago).

She spilled a tiny drop here and there among the quiet crush, but finally the pen was filled with potion.

The silence thickened.

Jenny tried to wriggle forward to sprinkle the 'STEPS' potion either on the lead rebel himself or on the ground beside him (she wasn't sure which would work, so planned to do both). However she found herself stuck fast among the tight crowd.

'We're far too far away, O'Flahertie. And I definitely can't touch the finished freedom document from here and get home. Can you lift me up, please?'

Her guide obligingly stooped to loop his hands together, exactly as he had done in the dim room off the university library all those years ago. 'Hop up, m'dear, then climb upon my shoulders.'

In a trice Jenny had invisibly done just that, with a clear – if worryingly distant – view of the silent rebel.

Sprinkle... SPRINKLE...sprinkle... SPRINKLE!

A large set of red steps rose. The rebel cleared his throat again and stepped up. The crowd roared.

Jenny was so relieved – and trying so hard to work out how to get home – that she only heard parts of the start of his speech.

'...summons her *children* to her flag and strikes for her *FREEDOMMMM...*'

'...having *resolutely* waited for the right MOMENT...'

I might make it if I jump really hard, but it will be touch and go, thought Jenny. *Hmmm. No, it's too risky. O'Flahertie will have to help out again.*

Her guide had continued to hold her feet firmly as she stood, surprisingly steadily, on his shoulders.

The people were listening intently to the proclamation (the speaker agonisingly turning bluer by the minute) as Jenny bent down and whispered her key question into O'Flahertie's ear.

'And why not, dear girl?' he replied. 'Indeed, it seems a fairly fair exchange. I shall see if I can... '

As he spoke, Jenny's backpack grew heavy and she almost toppled over with sheer surprise!

'Whoa, steady on, dear girl!'

Despite the crush, Jenny managed to shimmy back down O'Flahertie's back and open her rucksack. Her eyes widened with delight. *Yes!*

'Is this the means of propulsion you require, m'dear?' enquired O'Flahertie with a grin.

Tucked between the two university robes was the magic diving book!

'Thank you! If I stand on it, could you launch me off the top of your head?'

Jenny knew this could be tricky, but it was the only idea she could come up with under pressure.

Even though O'Flahertie had said he wouldn't oblige with any more magic, she tried one last try.

'Can you put a spell or potion on the book to make sure I reach the freedom document? Please?'

'Ah no, m'dear,' he replied softly but firmly. 'No more. This book itself is magic enough, believe me.'

Jenny swallowed a lump in her throat. *I'm going to really miss dear brilliant witty O'Flahertie!*

'Thank you for *everything*! I'll *never* forget you!'

'And vice versa, m'dear. Now, our exchange...?'

Jenny produced her second souvenir with a broad beam and handed it over.

'Thank you, dear girl,' he replied, twirling it between his fingers with a fond smile. 'I found it beautifully easy to write with, even on the run. Indeed, *especially* on the run.'

Jenny knew Jeremiah Gnome would be angry at her empty-handed return – but if anyone deserved a magic pen it was O'Flahertie, and that was that.

He helped her up onto his shoulders again.

Jenny took a last look around... and spotted a familiar horrible-stroke-handsome (blue) face in the rapt crowd – it was the blackmailer from the university!

'Did you ever write Horrible Dorian's essay?'

'Dear me *no*, my dear! I wrote something far, *far* better instead – and for my own good, not *his*!'

Delighted, Jenny placed the book on top of her guide's clever head and prepared to step up to the literary mark.

'One final parting shot, dear girl,' added O'Flahertie, his voice wobbling with emotion.

'You've been a pleasure – an absolute pleasure – and you must always remember this from dear old me: Be yourself; everyone else is already taken.'

With that, he let go of her feet as Jenny leapfrogged up and sprang off on her book launch...

The End of
The End

'U mphhhh!' Jenny rolled around for several dizzying rolls before managing to stop. Once wherever it was had stopped spinning, however, she could make out the familiar splodgy carpet of the Best Bedroom of All.

She was at the farmhouse, back in her own world.

'Aaaargghhhh. *Urrrr-GHHHH.*' For a moment Jenny had to figure out whether the noise was her or whether it was not.

It was not.

She quickly got up and opened the wardrobe door.

Jeremiah Gnome was sprawled on the knotty wooden floor inside, minus all the ancient brown suitcases from the beginning but with his beloved hatbox home sitting snug beside him.

His dinky typewriter lay on one side. Steam was rising from its worn keys.

The cranky Gnome in the Hatbox was clutching at his warty head and groaning.

'I'm *sooooo* exhausted,' he moaned. 'I've finished my fabulous masterpiece – but oh, the effort of fine-tuning my amazing craft has left me *tooootally drrrrained!*'

Jeremiah was lying on a bed of screwed-up balls of paper. They rustled and rolled as he wriggled and writhed with self-pity.

Jenny could make out the occasional word, or part of one at least, on several of the paper balls.

(As in: `'wolfhou'`, `'bat'`, `'fores'`, `'causwa'`, `'monk'`. *Hmmm.*)

Jeremiah gave Jenny several sneaky sideways looks as he moaned and groaned for ages.

She waited patiently, as she knew she must.

'Weee-*lllll*,' he drawled eventually, having run out of complaining steam. 'How did you get on *this* time?'

Jenny took a deep breath and was just about to–

'Actually,' – the gnome sat up and cut across her rudely – 'first things first: give me my two souvenirs.'

Jenny glared at Jeremiah, offended by his abrupt interruption. Surely he could have listened for just *a little bit* about her amazing times in history, especially since he had actually asked?

'I don't have them,' she retorted sharply,

tossing her hair. 'I had to use the special parchment to save the day for some important rebels and I gave the magic pen to my brilliant guide to get home.'

The gnome flapped and glared and huffed his disapproval. 'What, *again?* No souvenirs for me *AGAIN?*' he bellowed.

'I wanted to sign my fabulous masterpiece with that pen,' he bewailed. '*Aghhh!* This is *not good enough.* I think I may have to stop sending you on...'

Jenny's heart plummeted. Could Jeremiah really be saying he wouldn't help her go on any more fantastical journeys if she didn't give him a gift?

'Oh – erm – wait a moment, please,' she pleaded desperately, shrugging off her rucksack.

Jenny had only just thought of this, in a flash of pure panic: perhaps Jeremiah would accept the two university robes as souvenirs?

The bullet holes and rips weren't *that* bad, and she could offer to iron them...

She opened the rucksack, but with a sinking heart. *I think I'd have felt the robes when I landed. I doubt if they're in here any more. What am I going to do?*

As Jenny suspected, the robes had vanished.

However... tucked snugly into the bag's padded inside pocket... was... was an ink-spattered note wrapped around an oddly shaped bottle!

'My dear girl,' it read with a flourish. 'I trust you'll find this useful. Yours, O'Flahertie.'

Jenny was overcome. Even *after* their adventures, her generous guide was still looking out for her!

It was the red bottle marked 'STEPS'.

She offered it to the Gnome in the Hatbox with the warmest smile she could muster (which, on this occasion, was the chilly side of lukewarm).

'This will do nicely,' trilled Jeremiah, snatching the gift and flicking its contents towards the back of the wardrobe (whereupon a shimmery staircase began rising). 'See you next time. *Byeeeee!*'

He picked up his hatbox home and a thick sheaf of paper before starting up the steep steps.

Then, on the first one, he turned to Jenny with a malicious glint in his bulgy eyes.

'I almost forgot to read you some of my magnificent book,' he announced. 'Now listen carefully. Once upon a time, I... and then I... after that I... Oh, and because I... when I...*I...I...*'

Jenny woke up at home with a jump. The music for the television news was blaring. Mum was tutting that it was always bad news and they really shouldn't watch it any more.

Jenny reached for her computer pad on the sofa beside her. *Pleeeease don't let it all have been a dream. Pleeease. I've written an incredible Easter essay. I need it to be saved where I think it is.*

'Yay!' she whooped next. *Her essay was there!*

'Hello, Jenny dear,' said Mum. 'You dozed off after working so hard on your holiday homework and we decided not to disturb you. I think you should go to bed now, though.'

'I'll just check my essay really quickly, Mum, and then I'll go – I promise,' replied Jenny.

As she scrolled down... *well...* the very same events described in her Easter essay were unfolding on the television – including the rebel leader proclaiming the finished freedom document!

'Mum, *Dad*,' she began urgently. 'I was ther–'

'*Bed*, Jenny,' interrupted Dad firmly, but with a gentle smile for his curiously clever daughter. 'We'll research whatever it is tomorrow, I promise.'

But there was more to come – a *lot* more.

The rumpled book appeared on the screen, together with a *very* familiar bell tower.

'How...? Who...? Jenny's mouth fell open with surprise. '*What...?*'

Even the usually serious newsreader was smiling as she announced that a previously unknown volume of the world-famous book series had been found during restoration work in the campanile.

'It will go on display alongside the existing restored one in the university library,' she beamed.

The greenly writers had won the debate and got to keep the book in their own grand university after all!

The newsreader's face became full of awe as **'BREAKING NEWS'** scrolled across the screen.

'Oh!' Jenny gasped silently as a reddy-yellow scroll of parchment appeared next. '*Oh!*'

The original handwritten proclamation signed by the seven rebels had also been discovered hidden behind a statue in the university's bell tower during the renovation work!

'*Time for bed*, Jenny dear.'

Jenny reluctantly stood up, eyes glued to the television. The screen went fuzzy... and then... the inside of the post-office stronghold appeared, and...

... the camera zoomed in on an ornate portrait marked 'Wall of Fame'.

'There's... *he's*...' Jenny was lost for words.

In shimmery pride of place in this portrait was... *yes*... it was dear, dear O'Flahertie in his damaged robe, with the five green writers from the debate

glowing on either side of him.

As Jenny gazed admiringly at her guide, he lifted a quizzical eyebrow and winked...

The End

The History Bit

As I'm sure you have realised, the city in this Suitcases *book is Dublin, Ireland's wonderful capital. I took my inspiration from real events and people (although I had a lot of fun changing the course of history, too!). Here are some of the facts (and fictions) I used for my story:*

Oscar Fingal O'Flahertie Wills Wilde (1854–1900) was a brilliant Irish writer. One of his famous stories, A Picture of Dorian Gray, tells of a horribly handsome man obsessed with his looks. I put lots of Oscar/O'Flahertie's quotes in The Red-Letter Day as he guides Jenny through their crazy adventure. Oscar began studying in Trinity College, Dublin – where the (non-jelly!) bell tower is – in 1871.

The 1916 Easter Rising sparked Ireland's War of Independence against British rule, with Padraig Pearse reading the Proclamation of the Irish Republic outside the General Post Office (GPO) on April 24, 1916. The rebels were forced to surrender on April 29 and Padraig and the other brave signatories – Thomas J Clarke, Sean Mac Diarmada, Thomas MacDonagh, Eamonn Ceannt, James Connolly and Joseph Plunkett – were executed by firing squad at Kilmainham Gaol in Dublin in early

May. Cumann na mBan (the Irishwomen's Council) had a key role in 1916, with, among many others, Constance Markievicz and Maud Gonne to the fore. I hope you'll want to find out more about them all.

The Book of Kells is a sacred gospel penned by monks in Scotland and Ireland in the ninth century (the 806AD Viking raid on the Scottish isle of Iona did happen). The book was brought to Trinity College in 1661 after English tyrant Oliver Cromwell plundered and conquered Ireland. (It may have gone missing for a few years before that, so I decided to blame Cromwell!) A volume of the book is displayed in Trinity's majestic library in Dublin.

Finn McCool was a mythical Irish warrior who had a feud with Scottish giant Benandonner and, legend has it, built the Giant's Causeway in Northern Ireland to cross over to Scotland. I made up Fual (look up his cheeky name if you dare!). As for the Lough Ness Monster being real, who knows?

The debating writers on the English (blue-hued) side were Geoffrey Chaucer, Samuel Johnson, Sir Walter Raleigh, William Shakespeare and William Wordsworth. The Irish (greenly) ones were Samuel Beckett, Seamus Heaney, James Joyce, Bram Stoker and William Butler Yeats. (While I did poke fun at these talented writers for my book, please note that I do really admire them all a great deal!)

Finally... a red-letter day is one that's memorable for all the right reasons – hopefully like this book.

SP McArdle, April 24, 2016

The Thank-You Poem

For Oscar and Sophie and Matthew and Paul,
Lucia and Rachel, so focused them all...

...with Aoife and Mark – all viewed the fine art
and helped me decide who to draw for this part.

It was Kerry in Cape Town who took on the task
of pictures so vivid – no more could I ask.

She penned such great drawings for throughout this book,
with pens tucked in smartly wherever you look.

Then Audrey so gifted took over the pages,
like lightning she works... I would have been ages!

Anne's dedication plus Paddy's all-nighter
meant every last word was just that bit tighter.

So many have helped; I can't name each one –
but know that I'm grateful for all that you've done.

This book is dedicated to Rebeccas and Oscars, Padraigs and Saoirses – and to the rebel-yell children in all of us.

If you would like your name in the dedication of a *Suitcases* book please keep an eye on www.spmcardle.com

Thank you for reading The Red-Letter Day – I hope you enjoyed it.

I plan to set my next two *Suitcases* adventures in the awesome cities of Paris and New York – see you there!